MAC WALKER'S BE
The Collection

D.W. ULSTERMAN

2013

Other books available by D.W. Ulsterman:

MAC WALKER'S BETRAYAL
(Sequel to Mac Walker's Benghazi)

-DOMINATUS

-TUMULTUS

-THE SECOND OLDEST PROFESSION
The Collection

LUST. POWER. POLITICS.

http://dwulsterman.com

You will not fear the terror of night,
nor the arrow that flies by day,
nor the pestilence that stalks darkness,
nor the plague that destroys at midday.

A thousand may fall at your side,
ten thousand at your right hand,
but it will not come near you.

-Psalm 91: A soldier's prayer

I.

"This is Walker. Go ahead."

The call had come in on Mac's shadow cell. That meant work, which was a good thing because he was getting low on cash. His crew hadn't had a decent paying job since those three days in Albania, and that was almost four months ago. The economy was shit – and that shit was raining down on him and his crew just like it was everybody else.

"Hey Mac, this is Tilley. We have a program set up for you in Benghazi - at least two weeks worth. Interested?"

Ray Tilley had been Mac's primary mission securement contact for the last few years. They had known each other since the both of them were working out of the government's Project Icon program. Tilley brought Mac tough work, but that was the work that paid. Whatever they wanted done in Benghazi was going to be a pain in the ass – and that was the kind of job Mac loved.

"What's it pay Tilley?"

Tilley paused, leaving Mac's question unanswered.

"Tilley – you there? What's it pay?"

"Standard pay Mac – a thousand per day, plus expenses, which have already been estimated just north of thirty thousand."

Now it was Mac's turn to pause as he quickly did the calculations in his head. A thousand per day for two weeks would be $14,000 for himself and each of his men, plus the ten percent they were normally able to hold back for themselves from the expenses allotment.

For work in Libya, which at that time was possibly the single most fucked up part of the world, Mac decided the amount wasn't enough. He also figured Tilley already knew that.

"This isn't a standard mission Tilley. You said Libya, right? The place is crawling with the jihadists, there's got to be some Russians running around there trying to clean up all the evidence of the weapons dealings, or smuggling those weapons into Syria, the Saudis will have their people working the oil claims…we're talking some real serious shit going down over there. Plus, you know with this administration, however bad we think it is, it's gonna be worse."

Mac could hear Tilley shaking his head.

"Things are tight Mac – you know that. Our budget ain't what it used to---"

Mac cut him off. He knew Tilley needed him. Now it was just a matter of how much he was willing to pay.

"Fifteen hundred per, and I need payment for a forty eight hour prep, and a twenty four hour debrief – and at least forty thousand for expenses. So that's seventeen days total. I want those days guaranteed Tilley. No pushing us out before we're done. That works out to $25,500 for each of us, plus expenses. You provide the transport, the safe house, and the mission specs, and we take it from there.

That's the deal Tilley. You know we're the best. You want it done right – you have to pay right."

Mac waited for Tilley's approval. He knew fifteen hundred per day was pushing it, but he needed the money. They all did.

"Let me get back to you Mac. I'm gonna need the ok from Mardian. Give me an hour."

Stephen Mardian was the direct contact to the Senator Foreign Affairs Office, which in turn housed the shadow committee that hired people like Mac Walker to do things that needed to remain "off the books". Mardian was a sniveling, self-righteous and infuriatingly pompous asshole who Mac had never liked, and trusted less. That said, he had final approval of the operational budgets. It was for that reason and that reason alone that Mardian remained a necessary evil in Mac's ongoing work as a hired gun for the American government.

"That's fine Tilley. I'll be here."

Tilley's return call arrived in less than ten minutes.

"Ok Mac – you got the job. Your price. Mardian wants a sit down on this one though before you go. No exception."

In his head, Mac was screaming. A pre-mission sit down with Mardian was, thankfully, a rare thing. In fact, it had only happened twice in the last three years. Stephen Mardian generally thought himself to be above the fray – or at the very least, well beyond having to share the same room with the likes of Mac Walker.

"When does he want the sit down Tilley?"

"Tonight – 9:30 in the cellar."

The cellar was what Mac and Tilley called Mardian's place of business. A simple red-bricked three story office building near the 19th and G intersection the Mardian family had owned for nearly fifty years – the kind of old money power the D.C. politicians loved to rub elbows with. Mac had never been allowed to walk through the front door of the building though, and certainly was never invited during regular business hours. No, for people like him, the cellar was a "come in the back and see you downstairs" affair. In Mardian's eyes, Mac was the help – nothing more, and barely tolerated help at that.

Mac was about to end the call when he heard Tilley say something.

"Say again Tilley – I didn't have the phone to my ear."

"I need you to play nice this time Mac. I know you don't like Mardian. I don't either, but he's the link to the funding. He could move these operations to someone else. In fact, he already has here and there, so…just sit and listen. I'm sure the meeting will be brief."

Mac rolled his eyes – he hated playing politics with assholes like Mardian. All he wanted was a loaded weapon, a designated target, and payment for a job done right.

"Got it Tilley. Just smile and nod. As long as you keep it brief, I should be able to play dumb for at least ten minutes. After that, no guarantees. And if he starts quoting Shakespeare to me, I'll fucking kill him."

II.

Mac arrived at the back entrance to the cellar five minutes ahead of schedule. He parked his rented white sedan three blocks from the address and then walked, scanning the streets for any signs he was being followed. Having satisfied himself that he wasn't being watched, Mac quickened his pace as he entered the narrow alley that ran directly behind the Mardian building.

The former Navy SEAL saw the posted security detail well before they saw him. They were two large men, each of them no older than forty, dressed in matching navy blue suits with white shirts, well polished dark shoes, and red ties. They were Mardian's men – Tilley didn't hire out for security. He was more than capable of taking care of himself.

The taller of the two men stepped toward Mac as he revealed his right hand holding a simple Glock 21. Mac thought to himself how cheap Mardian must be to have his own security detail armed with such a basic weapon. Not that he had anything against the Glock, it was just so damn obvious – a cliché. Mac had long used his SEAL days SIG MK25 P226 that he had customized years ago to enhance its rapid fire capabilities. Watching the first, and then the second man move toward him, Mac was absolutely confident he could drop both of them before they fired a single shot.

"Sir, need you to stop there please."

Mac held his hands out to his sides, his palms facing the security detail.

"I'm here to see Tilley, downstairs. Have a 9:30."

The shorter man spoke into his left shirtsleeve while holding a hand to his right ear. Very Secret Service like, but without the actual training. Mac was laughing inside. These two were complete clowns. Clearly from some private security firm that was more interested in having their personnel look like they knew what they were doing, without actually knowing what they were doing. All show. In a real situation, that kind of style over substance gets people killed.

The taller man stood directly in front of Mac and looked him up and down.

"What's your name sir?"

Mac stared back into the taller man's eyes.

"Walker."

The other member of the security detail nodded to himself as he listened to his ear piece.

"Ok – he's approved. Let him through."

Mac offered both men a thin smile as he walked past them, pulling on the simple and surprisingly heavy red painted metal door that marked the entrance to the cellar. Just inside the doorway was another metal door to the left, and a dimly-list stairwell that led downward. Mac took the stairs.

Exactly twenty two steps later he faced someone Mac initially believed to be another member of Mardian's security team. This first impression quickly faded though as Mac realized the short, dark skinned, balding man looking back at him with well practiced, casual ease, was a far more capable and dangerous figure than either of the two men outside. This man wore a simple white, short sleeved dress shirt and blue jeans with tennis shoes. He was no more than five foot six, nearly a half foot shorter than Mac, and looked to be not quite sixty, making him some ten years older than Mac Walker.

Whoever the man was – he was a killer.

"Hello Mr. Walker. My name is Nigel. I need you to leave your sidearm here with me before allowing you inside."

Though the man's appearance suggested Middle Eastern descent, his accent was unmistakably British.

"And who are you with?"

Nigel's eyes glanced to Mac's upper left chest, where his handgun was holstered inside of his light grey and loose fitting military style jacket.

"Your firearm please, Mr. Walker. You can ask further questions once you are inside."

Mac removed his P226 and handed it to Nigel.

"Thank you Mr. Walker – as you already know, it's right through this door."

Nigel pointed to the entrance into the cellar, a thick, wooden, six panel door that had likely been part of the building's original construction decades earlier. Mac took the few steps to the door and pushed against the heavy, age-darkened brass handle, and walked inside.

The cellar's interior remained as Mac had last seen it. The unadorned walls were painted an off white, the entire twenty by twenty room illuminated by a single bulb that hung from the short ceiling. At the far end of the room was a simple oak desk, behind which sat Stephen Mardian. Tilley occupied a leather bound chair to the right of the desk, while a woman sat in a matching chair on the desk's left.

As he looked at the woman, the normally insistent and prevailing disdain Mac felt any time he saw Mardian, was quickly forgotten. The woman, whoever she might be, was incredibly beautiful. Mac Walker believed such beauty was always deserving of his full attention.

Tilley quickly rose from his seat as Mac entered the room, as did the woman. Mardian remained seated, his eyes hungrily scanning the woman's backside as she turned to face Mac.

"Hello Mac, I'd like to introduce you to Dasha Al Marri. She works with the United Nations.

The woman nodded her head at Mac, her large dark eyes appearing friendly, though guarded. She wore a long, light grey Gucci skirt, black belt, and matching black turtleneck. Mac didn't know what brand her high heeled shoes were, but they looked expensive. The woman clearly had money, and lots of it.

As Mac extended his right hand to shake hers, he continued to take in her impressive appearance. Likely in her thirties, with very thick dark black hair that she held back in a tight and professional looking bun, and flawless skin that complimented the high cheekbones of her face, Dasha Al Marri was possibly the most beautiful woman Mac had met. Given the three inch heels of her shoes, which made her almost as tall as him, Mac estimated her height to be five foot seven. He quickly noted no rings on her fingers, giving Mac hope that she was single. Mac Walker wasn't interested in a wife, but he was always interested in sharing a good time with a quality woman, and the one who stood in front of him now certainly represented that.

"It is nice to meet you Mr. Walker. I am looking forward to our doing some business together."

Her accent was similar to Nigel's – she must have spent considerable time in London.

"Nice to meet you as well Ms. Al Marri."

The woman's face broke into a wide and friendly smile, exposing perfectly proportioned white teeth.

"Please, you can simply call me Dasha."

Mardian had finally stood up from his chair and looked across the desk back at Mac, his deep set eyes and perpetually frowning mouth making him appear as dumb as Mac remembered.

"Hello Mac."

Mac turned his eyes away from Dasha to give Mardian a brief glance.

"Hey Steve."

Mac knew how much Mardian hated people calling him by the abbreviated version of his first name. The results, though predictable, remained entertaining.

"That is not my name Mac – it's Stephen Mardian. You are to call me Mr. Mardian. Am I making myself clear? I believe we've already had this very discussion before."

Mac shrugged back at Mardian.

"Did we? I have lots of discussions. Tough to keep track of all of them."

Mardian looked at Tilley, whose eyes were already pleading with Mac to behave himself.

"It's Mr. Mardian."

Mac allowed himself a thin smile as he motioned for Dasha to return to her seat.

"Sure thing Mr. Mardian. Got it."

Dasha and Tilley took their seats as Mac remained standing in between them. All three of them were looking back at Mardian who, after glaring back at Mac, sat down as well.

"Mr. Tilley, would you care to explain the mission parameters to Mac here? I have a 10:30 appointment with a congressman that I intend to keep."

Before Tilley could begin, Mac interrupted, pointing a finger back at Stephen Mardian.

"That would be Mr. Walker to you Mr. Mardian. If we're going to keep this all…professional like. Just saying…"

Mac spotted Dasha out of the corner of his eye trying to repress a smile. Mardian on the other hand, glared back at Mac again before looking over at Tilley, who in turn shifted uncomfortably in his chair.

"Ok, I'll be happy to get us started here Mr. Mardian. Mac, we need your team on the ground in Libya within seventy-two hours. As you know, with Gaddafi taken out, there's considerable chaos over there, power vacuums. We have the tribal leaders going after the kind of weapons that, well, we don't want those kinds of people capable of using that kind of firepower. There's your expected terrorist groups, some former military figures doing business, it all needs to be monitored and the more potentially dangerous elements shut down before it gets too out of hand. That said, we can't be sending in our military to do so. This was a U.N. run operation. At least officially. So---"

Mac interrupted Tilley again.

"So you need us to go in there unofficially. Sounds pretty standard Tilley. Why the face to face with Mardian on this? What else makes this operation different than the others?"

Ray Tilley looked over to Dasha, indicating he wanted her to provide some input. Mac turned his head to the left to look down at her, instantly appreciative of how much better looking she was than either Tilley or Mardian. Taking Tilley's cue, Dasha began to speak.

"What makes this task somewhat different Mr. Walker, are some of the particulars involved. Libya has been dealing in large arms trading for a very long time. Some believe there to be the remnants of nuclear capability. This has become a matter of importance for a great many of us who hope to see Libya's transition be as...smooth and unfettered by violence as possible."

Mac stared down at Dasha, looking past her beauty and trying to see what the motivation behind her involvement really was.

"And just what is your interest in this Dasha? Who do you represent?"

Dasha met Mac's stare calmly, her hands folding across her slender, crossed legs.

"My position with the United Nations involves a new approach Mr. Walker. For too long that institution has been viewed as something of a joke among the world's political class. There are those who feel it must...evolve. We must move beyond countless meetings and agendas, and idiotic statements that have no basis in reality, and are ultimately, non-binding. We have been pleased to see this view received rather warmly by the current American administration. Call it a more pro-active approach. We wish to give the United Nations real teeth, so that the world will come to realize if provoked, it can and more importantly will, bite back."

Inside his head, Mac could hear warning sirens beginning to sound.

"You think the United Nations needs to change? Become, what? More powerful? More...militaristic?"

Dasha remained exceptionally composed as she nodded her head.

"Yes, Mr. Walker. Think of it as a new beginning for the organization. A New United Nations, if you will."

Now the warning sirens in Mac's head were on full alert, blaring loudly.

"You want me and my crew to go into Libya to represent this new approach by the United Nations? No way. We work for the American government. I'm former military, we all are. All due respect Dasha, but I can't stand the U.N., and I'm sure calling it the "New" United Nations won't change that one bit. They've never been nothing but a bunch of pencil pushing bureaucrats always complaining about how shitty America is, or how evil our military is, or that the earth's too cold, or too hot and how if only we didn't drive cars or heat our homes it would make everything all better. Bullshit. No way. I ain't doing the work of the United Nations. Sorry Tilley – you're gonna have to get someone else for this one. Not interested."

Mardian's voice slithered across his desk, dripping venom.

"You already agreed to do the job Mac. Tilley told me. If you don't want the job, fine. You won't get this job. You won't get any job. Ever. You'll be doing security at a fucking Walmart, you arrogant asshole!"

Tilley attempted to intervene as he saw Mac's eyes turn dangerous while staring back at Mardian.

"This is an important operation Mac. We've agreed to pay you what you asked for, and if this goes well, I know there's going to be a lot more work coming your way. This would be very good for your career Mac. You ain't getting any younger. Time to start saving your pennies, right?"

Mac ignored Tilley, looking back down at Mardian who was beginning to wither under his gaze. Dasha rose from her chair to look at Mac directly.

"Please Mr. Walker, I have reviewed your file. You are absolutely the right person for this operation. Mr. Mardian is correct, there will be more work available to you after satisfactory completion of the Libyan operation."

Mac's eyebrows raised slightly as he looked away from Dasha and down at Tilley.

"She has access to my file? I thought we were off the books Tilley? How does someone from the U.N. have access to MY file? Access to any record of what we've been doing? What the hell is going on here?"

"I am connected Mr. Walker, to more than simply the United Nations. That is my official capacity. Like you, I have what you might like to call, an unofficial capacity as well. Access to your file is not really the issue here. What is at issue is our need to have you take this assignment. Would you consider an additional one hundred thousand dollars in payment Mr. Walker? Half up front? You and your men could certainly use that kind of money, right?"

Mardian began to object, complaining that Mac was already being paid well for his potential services. This caused Dasha to hold up her hand to Mardian as she ripped through his objection.

"Mr. Mardian, I would like you to simply sit there now and shut up. I don't care for you, and neither does Mr. Walker here, and your behavior suggests our feelings are not without merit."

In Washington D.C., it was a very rare thing for anyone to speak to Stephen Mardian as Dasha did at that moment. His personal contact list was a collection of the most influential figures within that city's mighty corridors of power. And yet, much to Mac's amazement, Mardian's eyes lowered and he said nothing, causing Mac to silently wonder who this Dasha really was.

"Now, Mr. Walker, I would like to invite you to my D.C. residence as my personal guest. Let us have dinner and discuss your involvement in this pending operation further. I'm a notorious night owl, so for me a late dinner is the rule rather than the exception. Do you accept?"

For the first time since arriving at the cellar Mac felt nervous. Part of him wanted to tell the woman to go to hell. Another part of him screamed to accept the offer and have dinner with her. It only took a few brief seconds for that other part to overcome his indecision.

"Sure – I'll have dinner with you. Are you cooking?"

Dasha gave her beautiful head a brief shake.

"No Mr. Walker, the meal will have already been prepared. That will leave us more time to talk,
and get to know each other better."

The warning sirens in Mac's head were sounding again...

III.

By the time Mac and Dasha emerged from the cellar, Nigel already had the car ready to take them to Dasha's residence, the location of which remained unknown to Mac.

The vehicle was a black, S550 Mercedes sedan. It was a car common to the political dignitaries who permeated Washington D.C., though Mac was able to ascertain this one had been upgraded with an impressive integrated security package. The rear door Mac opened for himself was much heavier than the standard S550, indicating the shell in shell armoring and attack resistant glass. The car felt as solid as any vehicle Mac had sat in, including a limousine that had once been used for the presidential motorcade.

"This is quite a car Dasha. You're either a lot more important than your work with the United Nations suggests, or very rich and very paranoid."

Dasha slid gracefully into the left rear seat of the Mercedes as Nigel closed her door and then positioned himself behind the wheel. Looking over at Mac, Dasha gave a slight smile at his comment regarding the car before staring ahead as Nigel drove slowly down the alley before turning right onto G Street.

"Perhaps I am all that and more Mr. Walker."

Both Mac and Dasha remained silent as Nigel drove the Mercedes past the massive IMF building and east along G Street before going right onto Virginia Avenue. Within another minute Mac was able to determine where they were heading.

"You stay at the Watergate Complex?"

Dasha's eyes remained looking directly ahead of her as she replied to Mac.

"Yes - Watergate West, when I am here in Washington D.C., which is as little as possible. I despise this place and its people even more. I much prefer New York, London, and as much as possible, Dubai."

Mac nodded, trying to keep the still mysterious woman talking.

"I can relate to that. Too many political zombies in D.C. and not enough real people. The place gives me the creeps."

Dasha turned her head slightly toward Mac as her slender fingered right hand reached out to rest itself on Mac's left forearm.

"And where is it that you come from Mr. Walker? Your file said Louisiana, is that right?"

Mac wasn't sure if Dasha actually wanted to know where he was born and raised, or if she was simply reminding him that she knew a lot more about him than he did her.

"I'm just a simple Louisiana boy, that's right."

Dasha gave Mac's arms a gentle squeeze and smiled, her white teeth flashing in the dim light of the Mercedes' back seat.

"Oh, I know you are far from simple Mr. Walker, and quite dangerous if need be."

Nigel pulled the car into the underground garage of the Watergate West complex, home to many of the capitol's most prominent power brokers for decades. The building offered location, security, and access – all the essential components for those demanding to rise through the ranks of the Washington D.C. hierarchy.

Mac noted the elevator rose to the thirteenth floor of Watergate West – the top floor, home to the most expensive and exclusive apartments in one of the most expensive and exclusive buildings in the area.

As the elevator door opened, a gun appeared in Nigel's hand as he moved in front of Dasha, looking down both ends of the well lit hallway. Only after determining nobody else was nearby did he step completely out of the elevator and allow Dasha to walk closely behind him. Dasha appeared bored by Nigel's protective practice, indicating she had been doing this very routine for some time already. Mac on the other hand, made note of Nigel's every movement. The small man had been well trained. His handgun was a Browning High Power, a very old school British service weapon, leading Mac to believe Nigel had likely been affiliated with one of the Brit's Special Forces groups. If so, that made him both well trained, and smart. Even though several years older than Mac, Nigel would likely still prove a formidable opponent.

Dasha stopped in front of a door at the far end of the hall and input a security code into what Mac knew to be a vault door system. While the door appeared to be a normal residential door on the outside, it was actually constructed of bare reinforced steel, offering a resident considerable security. As the door swung inward to the residence, Nigel was again the first to enter the room with Dasha following behind.

The apartment was both spacious, though it contained almost no furnishings. A basic kitchen area was to the left of the entranceway, a large living area that had only a small dark clothed couch and matching chair, and then French doors to an outside balcony that overlooked the Potomac River. Opposite the kitchen was a narrow hallway that Mac assumed led to the bedrooms.

Dasha turned to Mac as she gestured with her left arm and hand toward the living area.

"I apologize for the scarcity of furnishing Mr. Walker. As I said, I don't spend much time here, and don't feel the need to make it more comfortable. This apartment has been in my family since the buildings' construction some years ago. Please, have a seat while Nigel warms up the meal.

Nigel was already removing plates of prepared food from the kitchen's refrigerator and placing them in the microwave as Dasha sat on the couch. Mac was already sitting in the accompanying chair.

"Nigel prepares my meals each morning. All they require is a bit of warming up. He is an incredible cook – spoils me terribly. We're not here to talk of food though, are we Mr. Walker? I have a job needing your particular skills, and very much hope you will accept the assignment. Can I count on you to do so Mr. Walker?"

Mac could smell the food Nigel was warming up in the kitchen and realized he hadn't eaten in several hours. He was hungry.

"How about I get some food in me first and we talk after that?"

Mac found Dasha's frown to be as beautiful as her smile.

"I do hope you don't intend to dine and dash on me Mr. Walker."

Dasha rose from her seat while speaking to Nigel.

"We'll take our meal in my bedroom Nigel. Thank you."

Nigel simply nodded his head as he began plating the just warmed food. Mac in turn found himself following Dasha down the hallway, wondering to himself how much more the beautiful woman was willing to pay to secure his services for the mission.

Unlike the main living area of the apartment, Dasha's bedroom was a full on display of luxury and wealth. From the massive and ornate dark leather bound Armani king sized bedframe and matching chairs, the handcrafted dark stone fireplace, to the incredibly intricate and colorful oriental carpet, the room represented no pretense, but rather real and significant financial means.

Another door opened onto a private balcony, similar to that offered in the main room but smaller. Dasha opened that door and stepped outside, the still warm and humid summer evening air quickly filling the air conditioned room.

"This is my favorite part of the residence Mr. Walker. I can just make out the Georgetown Cathedral from here, and the river's waters below look so dark and mysterious."

Mac remained inside the bedroom, just outside the balcony area where Dasha stood leaning against the railing as Nigel entered the room and placed two plates of food and two glasses of water atop a small dark, solid wood trestle table and matching chairs that sat directly in front of the fireplace.

Dasha had already re-entered the room, though she left the door to the balcony open.

"Thank you Nigel. Please close the door behind you. I won't be needing you anymore this evening."

Nigel glanced at Mac briefly before looking back at Dasha and nodding his head. He closed the door behind him as she had requested.

"How long has Nigel been providing your security?"

Dasha sat in one the chairs and began picking at her food – slices of lightly buttered summer squash, roasted tomatoes, and steak tartare with white truffle oil. She paused to consider Mac's question.

"It's been almost seven years now. He's both very good and very loyal. Let's not spend our time talking of Nigel though Mr. Walker. I need your assurance you intend to accept the assignment in Libya. Please, sit down and eat while we discuss it."

Mac sat opposite Dasha and inhaled the tartare in one bite, his stomach already growling for more.

"You appear to be rather hungry Mr. Walker."

Mac nodded as he worked his way through the roasted tomatoes and squash.

Dasha's eyes twinkled as she looked back at Mac over her water glass while taking a slow drink.

"Would you like some wine Mr. Walker?"

Mac was eyeing the remaining steak tartare on Dasha's plate.

"Yeah – and you can go ahead and pass that steak over my way too if you ain't gonna finish it."

Dasha laughed as she stood up, and Mac found the sound almost as satisfying as the minced and seasoned steak.

"It is so nice to spend time with a man and not another preening politician Mr. Walker. Or worse yet, a babbling bureaucrat from the United Nations!"

With a push of a button, a section of the wall to the right of the fireplace opened up to reveal a fully stocked bar, including several bottles of wine.

"I prefer a nice, deep, red wine at night Mr. Walker. How about you?"

Mac was now scraping the rest of Dasha's roasted tomatoes onto his plate.

"Sure – pour it and I'll drink it."

After opening a bottle of wine, Dasha filled two glasses and moved slowly across the room toward the balcony.

"I'll be just outside Mr. Walker. Please join me when you're ready."

Mac smiled to himself. He had already decided to do the Libya assignment, even if it meant working for some group affiliated with the United Nations. Their money would spend the same as anyone else's. He was now increasingly certain he'd be working a little late night fun into the deal as well, and judging from the way Dasha had been looking him over, she seemed more than interested in offering as much. When the lights went out, we all wanted company – rich or poor, it didn't matter.

The fact she was also incredibly attractive made it all the better...

IV.

Mac woke to find Dasha already in the bathroom and Nigel putting breakfast on the same small table in front of the bedroom fireplace he had served dinner at the night before. Glancing at his Resco Patriot watch, Mac saw it was just past 0700.

"Good morning Mr. Walker. I assume you have accepted the assignment then?"

Nigel's demeanor suggested minor annoyance at finding Mac waking up in Dasha's bed.

Mac put his hands behind his head and smiled back at Nigel.

"Probably. Gonna wait and see what kind of breakfast you serve up. Could be the deal maker or deal breaker right there."

Nigel tipped his head down slightly to the left and then exited the room, closing the door behind him.

Mac rose from the bed and walked unclothed to the table of food. Each plate had a small serving of fresh fruit, two pieces of lightly buttered wheat toast, and a dollop of yogurt. Two cups of dark, freshly brewed coffee and two glasses of orange juice had also been placed alongside the plates.

Mac picked up a cup of coffee and took a slow sip, relishing the rich quality of the brew. Behind him he heard Dasha approaching from the bathroom and turned around to greet her with a smile. She seemed unfazed by his lack of clothing, though she had wrapped herself in a very comfortably looking cream colored cotton robe.

"I see you've already discovered Nigel's coffee. There are all the essentials you will need in the bathroom Mac, including a toothbrush, soap, hair products, and the like. Please take your time. When you are in the shower I can have staff clean and press your clothes and they will be done by the time you're ready."

Mac grabbed a piece of toast and made quick work of it, washing it down with another gulp of coffee.

"No thanks on the clothes. I'll just brush my teeth, get dressed, and be on my way Dasha. I'll take the assignment. Have to get a hold of my crew and go over the details with them, and then give final confirmation to Tilley. He handles all the transport and related items. We can be operational within twenty four hours."

Dasha appeared pleased by Mac's acceptance, smiling slightly as she walked toward him.

"That is very good to hear Mr. Walker, very good indeed. I am pleased to see our time together last night did not…lessen your enthusiasm for the mission."

Mac felt familiar stirrings, and knew if he didn't get moving, he would likely be spending another hour inside of Dasha's room. Looking again at his watch, he quickly decided he had another hour to spare and ran toward the large bed, jumping back into its covers. Mac looked back at Dasha as he leaned across the bed, his hand patting the space next to him.

"Might need just a little more convincing. That is, as long our time together last night didn't lessen your enthusiasm for me."

Dasha's eyes devoured Mac hungrily, as her robe fell to the floor.

"Not at all Mr. Walker. Not at all…"

Mac's estimate of time turned out to be somewhat off. He didn't leave Dasha's bedroom for nearly ninety minutes.

Nigel drove him back to what was a common meeting place for Mac and his crew – the Hillside Pub, a small bar owned by a former Marine Mac had served with years ago. His name was Carlos Diaz. Born to Mexican immigrant parents, Diaz had been a good soldier, and remained an even better man. Mac trusted him with his life.

Mac had already called ahead that morning to let Diaz know he would be using the private back room of the bar for a meeting. As always, Carlos said it was no problem – the room was theirs and nobody would bother them.

"Nice to see you Mac. Hope things are well."

Diaz shook Mac's hand warmly. He was just over forty years old, a few inches shorter than Mac's six foot height, with a slight paunch that had developed in recent years. Carlos was a perpetually grateful man – grateful for being born in America, grateful for the life the military afforded him, and now most of all, grateful to be happily married with two beautiful and healthy daughters and providing for them with his own business.

"Sorry it's a bit early Carlos – hope I'm not putting you out."

Carlos waived away Mac's concerns and guided him past the few booths and bar stools of the pub's main room toward a hallway at the back where the private room was located.

"Not at all Mac. You know that – welcome to use my place anytime."

The small room was low ceilinged and had a narrow oak table that ran down the room's center that offered enough room for four chairs on each side of the table. There were no windows. Lighting came from a floor lamp that had been placed in the right corner which Carlos left on 24/7.

Mac thanked Carlos as the he closed the door and then sat down at the table to begin making his calls to his crew. Within a few minutes, all of them had been contacted and were on their way to Mac's location. They knew the drill – when an assignment came in, they were to drop everything and respond immediately.

Jack Thompson was the first to arrive. The tallest of Mac's crew, with a blonde haired crew cut and square jaw, Jack had been born and raised in Alabama. He had been a high school football standout, but a knee injury turned away the college recruits and Jack enlisted in the military a few months after graduation. He was now forty two years old, having worked military contracts with Mac for the last seven years. His brother James was Secret Service – did the presidential detail for Obama during the first term before being suddenly reassigned to a hole in the wall post in North Dakota of all places. In recent years, Jack had grown increasingly agitated over the direction of the American government, and would take any opportunity to share those views with others. Despite the occasional annoyance of that sharing, he remained a very capable soldier, and most important, was someone who kept his wits about him when the shit hit the fan.

Mac rose from his seat to shake Jack's hand, then motioned for the big man to sit down. Jack already knew Mac wouldn't go into the details until the rest of them had arrived, so he simply sat there silently.

Jay Minnick was the next to enter the small room. Minnick was the shortest of the four men that made up Mac's team. He wore steel rimmed glasses that, along with his neatly trimmed brown hair, gave his face the appearance of an accountant, though anyone who saw Minnick shoot a rifle would soon realize the kinds of numbers Minnick was primarily involved with were kill shots. Mac was a very capable shooter himself, but Minnick was something special – the most accurate sniper Mac had ever seen. The fact Minnick was also tech savvy made him that much more valuable to the team. It was Minnick who helped deliver Mac's first assignments – his father was a former Congressman with long standing ties to high ranking military contacts.

The last to arrive, as usual, was Benjamin Williams, known by everyone as Benny. Benny came in as he always did, with a wide smile and a hug for Mac. The man was perpetually happy. He came from upstate New York, the youngest son of a longtime military family. One of his grandfathers had been one of the Tuskegee Airmen, the first African American military pilots who had fought so valiantly during World War II. Now in his mid-forties, Benny would likely still be in the military if not for an incident involving a superior officer and a bar fight. The officer was noted for being a mean drunk, and for whatever reason, on that night he took it upon himself to harass Benny and a group of enlisted men who were sitting at a table enjoying several rounds of drinks and jokes. Benny allowed the officer to hit him twice before he hit back. Likely unknown to that officer, Benjamin Williams was among the most highly trained hand to hand combat members within the entire United States military. He was obsessed with his martial arts training, and was the one member of the team Mac would not want to tangle with personally in a one on one fight. That officer was literally scraped off the floor of the bar, and three days later, Benny faced a court martial, learning then that the officer's father was a retired three star general who had made some calls and wanted "That Black boy who kicked the shit out of my son to be finished." That led Benny to eventually meet up with Mac, and he had been perhaps the single most dedicated member of the team besides Mac himself, for the last six years. Benny was also the only one of the four of them who was married and a father.

"Ok gentleman, we have ourselves an assignment, and I think you'll be pleased with the pay. Tilley got us fifteen hundred per day and a twenty one day guarantee with another forty thousand for expenses."

Minnick quickly did the math in his head.

"So that's $25,500 for each of us, plus whatever we can scrape off of the forty thousand from the expenses amount."

Mac nodded to Minnick.

"That's right – but it gets better. We are also getting an additional hundred thousand."

Benny let out a long, slow whistle.

"Why the extra hundred grand Mac? That doesn't sound like Mardian. Who we working for on this one?"

Mac left Minnick's questioned unanswered for a moment as he glanced at Benny.

"We're going through Tilley like usual. The funding is connected to someone connected to the U.N. though. I'm not sure of the specifics, but Tilley seems ok with it, so…I figured we would be too."

Jack's expression told Mac all he needed to know – the big man wasn't happy. Not one bit.

"Shit Mac – the United Nations? Since when do we do work for them? You really think this is a good idea?"

Minnick quickly interjected.

"Jack, we're talking fifteen hundred a day plus we get to split another hundred thousand between us. I could use the money, and know you could too. Who cares where it comes from, right? As long as we're still the good guys, I could give a shit."

Mac continued to look over at Benny, who remained silent. Mac knew the normally outgoing man was thinking the United Nations angle over very carefully. Finally, Benny asked a question.

"Where's the location Mac?"

Mac again paused briefly before answering.

"Libya."

Jack's concerns intensified immediately, his Alabama drawl extending his expression.

"Ohhhh shit, Mac. Fucking Libya? That place is God's asshole. What the hell we doin' going into that firefight?"

Mac looked at Jack, his jaw setting as he sensed his eyes flaring slightly.

"Because that's the assignment Jack. That's where the money is taking us. You want to sit this one out? Fine – your call. It always is. Me…I'm going in. That's what we do. That's our operation. We do the things the government wants done…unofficially. You suddenly developed a problem with that?"

Jack Thompson was not easily intimidated, but his respect for Mac both as an operational leader, and a man who could prove most unforgiving when crossed, gave Jack pause.

"I'm not saying no on the assignment Mac. Just…just wondering how it came about. Libya is a mess right now. You've got to be hearing the same things I am. It's like they went and pulled the plug without thinking first about how they were gonna get around in the dark. Just one big ass clusterfuck. And you know my feelings about this administration. I don't trust nothin' that's had their hands on it."

Mac shrugged.

"And that's just the kinds of places that we get called into Jack. Our job is to bring our own little version of peace and happiness to that…what was it you called it? God's asshole."

Benny rapped his knuckles on top of the table.

"I'm in Mac. That kind of money…just too good to pass up. Twenty one days? Shit, we can do that in our sleep."

Minnick nodded.

"Me too Mac. I'm in. Ready to go."

That left Mac looking back at Jack, who in turn rolled his eyes.

"Fine. Guess I can't let you little shits go off and get killed 'cause I wasn't there to keep an eye on you. Fuck."

Mac stood up from the table.

"Ok, I'll confirm with Tilley and we meet tomorrow morning at the hangar for a 0600 departure."

Mac waited for the others to exit the room and then reached into a pocket and retrieved two clean, crisp, one hundred dollar bills which he left on the table. Carlos always refused payment for the use of the room, and Mac always left two hundreds each time before leaving. The man was raising a family after all, and in this world, that was about the hardest job there was.

V.

The hangar was a private airport some twenty miles from downtown D.C., used primarily by the political elite and movers and shakers who wanted to get into and out of the capitol with as little notice as possible. It was Minnick who, through a suggestion from his Congressman father, introduced Mac to the facility. Though a private facility, its runway was long enough to accommodate a 747 if needed, and many times during the year, it did just that. There were rumors members of the Saudi royal family used the airport to leave the United States within hours of the September 11th, 2001 terrorist attacks.

Mac glanced at his watch, noting the others should be arriving within the next ten minutes. He saw the Gulfstream III that Tilley had been using to transport them from the hangar location the last two years. It was a military grade jet that had a range of just over four thousand miles at a cruise speed of over five hundred miles an hour. It was one of countless items that were part of massive appropriation bills that allowed multiple off the books programs like theirs to exist.

The Gulfstream's pilot was a guy Mac had come to simply call Captain Bob. Robert Hazelbrook was a retired Air Force pilot who, as Tilley had told it to Mac years ago, had been handling transport services for these types of operations for nearly twenty years. Mac was shocked when Tilley had recently informed him Captain Bob turned seventy.

Hazelbrook walked across the narrow runway toward Mac, stopping in front of him to shake his hand. His full head of closely cropped dark hair remained almost entirely free of gray. Physically, the still lean retired Air Force pilot could have easily passed for a man twenty years younger. Mac was hopeful that as the years passed, he would remain as well preserved as Captain Bob.

"Hello Mac. Already received the destination instructions this morning – going to be landing you boys in a place called San Vito. Haven't flown into there since Kosovo back in...hell, 1999 or so."

"Who runs the San Vito facility? Is it American military?"

Captain Bob shook his head.

"No – used to be. We gave it over to the Italians a decade ago, and then they handed it to the United Nations. Far as I know, what little use it sees now is as a hub for humanitarian projects. At least that's the official word. Our going there would suggest it's being used for a whole lot of other things too."

Mac assumed Dasha had access to the airport then, and had helped to coordinate its use for the current assignment. Whether that was a good or bad thing, he wasn't yet sure. While he enjoyed the time he had spent with Dasha, he remained unconvinced of being able to fully trust her. Neither of them shared much personal information with each other last night or this morning.

Captain Bob looked up as Tilley's black SUV parked adjacent to the runway. Tilley and the remainder of Mac's team exited the vehicle. Mac could already tell that Jack remained more tense than normal regarding the mission, the big man's brow furrowed as he made his way to where Mac and Captain Bob stood.

Tilley nodded to Mac and the captain and then gave the team a quick briefing as he always did right before departure.

"Ok gentleman, half of the additional hundred thousand has already been deposited electronically into your blind accounts, as Ms. Al

Marri promised to Mac yesterday. Your forty thousand expense funds will be waiting for you upon arrival at the San Vito facility. You'll be met there by a man named Angelo Moretti. He's my direct contact there, and he'll be the one securing your passage into Libya. He has all the credentials ready to go. He's also coordinating with our Libyan contact for your weapons and the safe house. The actual assignment parameters and communications instructions will be at the safe house. Mac, please confirm your arrival there ASAP, and then do twenty four hour updates after that per standard procedure. That's it then, unless there are any questions?"

Mac looked to the other three in his crew before shaking his head back at Tilley.

"We're good Tilly – ready to fly out of here."

Captain Bob nodded, and began making his way back to the Gulfstream.

"Lift off in ten boys. See you aboard."

Mac shook Tilley's hand and then took several steps toward the jet before pausing when he heard Tilley call him back.

"Hey – be careful on this one. There's a lot going on there. Libya has the attention of some real nasty fucks. You need to be on your game. I want you all coming back safe, ok?"

Mac gave Tilley a quick thumbs up before jogging over to the Gulfstream and then bounding up the boarding platform steps. Jack, Minnick and Benny were already onboard.

Twenty minutes later they were shooting across the clear morning summer skies of Maryland, and soon after, out over the blue waters of the Atlantic. Captain Bob's voice calmly called out over the interior cabin's intercom system, indicating they would be arriving at the San Vito airport in just over eight hours.

Their Libyan mission had begun.

VI.

A few hours into the flight and Mac found himself peering over at Jack, watching as the big man looked out the small window next to his seat.

"You ok Jack? Feeling alright enough about the assignment?"

Jack's blue eyes glanced back at Mac as he took a deep breath, gathering his thoughts before responding to Mac's question.

"No Mac…not gonna lie to you and say everything's good. It's not. Hasn't been for a while now. I'm telling you, telling all of you, things are getting weird. This whole Libya bullshit, how it all went down, I don't like it. Don't like flying into it. Not one bit."

While Jack Thompson had become increasingly paranoid about the American government in recent years, Mac considered him intelligent enough to still differentiate between a real threat and nonsense. If he was sincerely worried about going into Libya, Mac wanted to know why. He moved seats to allow him to look directly back across at Jack.

"Ok then – tell me what you think is going on Jack. I want to hear it."

Jack folded his well muscled arms across his chest, looking at Mac in silence for nearly a minute before proceeding.

"How much do you know about how Gaddafi was taken out Mac? Did you bother looking into it before accepting this assignment?"

Mac's pride was hurt a bit by Jack's accusation. Of course he informed himself of some of the particulars – he wasn't an idiot.

"Yeah, Tilley broke it down for me. For the most part."

Jack shook his head as his eyes returned to looking out the window.

"Shouldn't depend so much on Tilley's version of things Mac. Do your own homework – connect the dots."

"You saying Tilley can't be trusted Jack?"

Jack shook his head again.

"No, I'm not saying that. He gets his information through his Congressional contacts. The Senate…whatever. I don't trust those fuckers anymore than I trust Mardian, and I know you don't trust him."

"Ok Jack, then you give me your version of Libya. Why are you so worried about this assignment? It's not the first shithole we've gone into. What makes this one any different than the others?"

Jack's arms remained crossed over his chest as he tilted his head back against the top of his seat.

"Do you know how the take down was started? Gaddafi's fall? What was the event that got that rolling?"

Mac shook his head.

"He was a dictator and people had enough. I know we had operatives there pushing for the protests, helping get things rolling. That's nothing new. We've been doing that kind of thing for decades."

Jack appeared to ignore Mac's response.

"It was the alleged arrest of a man named Fergi Tahbell. A human rights activist in Libya with strong ties to organizations in the United Nations, throughout Europe, and the United States. Within hours of his arrest, there were people marching in Benghazi. That is where this thing originated – that is where our operatives were focused. The protests were bullshit. Staged. Their purpose was to incite protest throughout Libya, but what was going on in Benghazi, was highly controlled Mac. Every minute of it was orchestrated. Within a week of the Benghazi protests, the United Nations is locking down Gaddafi, moving for a war crime tribunal, the whole nine yards. It goes down fast, Mac. You get that? How fast it all happened? How smoothly? What does that tell you?"

Mac pondered Jack's question for a brief moment. Certainly the United Nations wasn't thought of as a smooth, quick responding organization. Not normally, anyways.

"That would tell me it was operational, like you said. Not some random protest event that few in size, but something that had been planned."

Jack nodded back at Mac.

"Of course, we know it when we see it, right? We've been part of those things, right? Egypt, Iraq, it's what we do. Libya was different though Mac. We weren't the lead in that. We were taking orders from somewhere else. The United States was deferring to the United Nations. The administration took a back seat. Since when does that happen? And why?"

Mac wasn't sure - though he couldn't disagree with anything Jack had said to this point.

Jack continued his version of what really happened during the fall of Gaddafi.

"Ok, so you have this human rights activist arrest story. He wasn't arrested Mac. He was placed into custody by U.N. operatives working in Benghazi. They had control of that prison complex. He was kept there willingly. He was never in any danger. The whole thing was a ruse, and Benghazi was the focal point. Not Tripoli – Benghazi. I'll bet you my full share Mac, that's where we're headed. We won't be camping out in Tripoli for this assignment – it'll be Benghazi. And that's a big reason why I'm not feeling right on this thing. That place…for people like us, that place is hell."

Mac was about to speak but Jack held up a hand to cut him off.

"Let me keep going with this Mac. There's more – a lot more."

Almost all of our initial media coverage of what was going down in Benghazi and soon after, the rest of Libya, came from a guy named Abdallas Dahnat. He's based in the United States, another human rights organization, funded by a lot of the same progressive groups that got Obama elected. In fact, he was meeting with high ranking White House officials just two weeks before the Benghazi riots. He was the one who was spinning the arrest story at the very start. In fact, this guy was calling out Gaddafi big time months before the protests in Benghazi began. He was paving the road, getting everything ready to go operational. He's plugged into the far left media in America, all the progressive community organizing type groups. And I'm pretty sure he's CIA Mac. At least a lot of what he does, in some capacity, he's CIA by way of the U.N. He's one of ours, and more importantly, he's one of theirs.

So follow me here...we have the Benghazi protests heating up, the United Nations moving quick to go after Gaddafi, the European Union is doing the same thing, but the American government seems to staying pretty quiet about all of it. Why is that? Simple, we have to give the protests the appearance of being genuine and not manufactured by us, right? At the same time though, we're already arming the protesters, who are actually tribal militants. We are arming them and working directly with United Nations operatives to make that happen. Not working with the United Nations though Mac, but taking our orders from them. Get it? The United States is taking direction from people affiliated with the United Nations to topple a government. We've taken out governments before – but since when do we do it on the orders of the United Nations?"

Mac sat silent, not certain of how much of what Jack believed to be true, actually was. Mac didn't doubt Jack's sincerity in what he was saying, but the fact he just spent a night making love to a woman who described to him the need for a "New United Nations", an organization that was to have the power to enforce its demands upon the world, certainly left Mac with an increasingly uneasy feeling. Maybe Jack was right. Maybe this assignment they were now involved in was part of something much bigger, and much more influential than any of them could fully comprehend.

Jack wasn't quite done, as he now leaned forward in his seat, his blue eyes narrowing as he focused on convincing Mac what he was telling him about Libya was true.

"We were sending drones by the dozens every day over to Libya Mac, bombing the hell out any group with even the slightest inclination to defend Gaddafi. So while our president was saying publicly there were no troops in Libya, the fact is, we sent all those drones over there and took over the skies, which allowed the militants who we had armed, to win the ground. It was a test run for drone power Mac, and the United Nations was very interested in how it worked out.

That's just the surface though Mac. The real deal here is why all of this went down. Who was to gain from Gaddafi being taken out? Why did this plan happen at all? The media reports didn't say anything about Gaddafi's ties to world leaders. Not much anyways. He was tight with Britain, France, Russia, and more recently, the United States. And he was getting rich off of it. Billions of dollars in oil sales. Enough to shift the market if he wanted. And some of those billions went to the same governments I just listed off. And more governments than just those – a lot more. The United Nations could give a shit about human rights. That's just a term used to allow programs to be put in place to shift money, and control people. It's all a scam Mac. A huge, global scam.

So if all these other governments were ok with Gaddafi, and could care less about what was happening to the Libyan people, why all of a sudden a rush to take him out? Who has that kind of pull? Who has that kind of power and influence that the leaders of Britain and France would jump so quickly onto the anti-Gaddafi bandwagon? So you know who Gaddafi was in almost constant communication with right before he was killed Mac? Have you had that information told to you? Did Tilley bother to mention it?"

Mac shook his head.

"Gaddafi was talking directly with Assad. They pulled the satellite links, Mac. Let that sink in. Assad. Syria. What do we have going on there right now? It's the same damn thing as Libya – at least that's what's being attempted. But Gaddafi gave him the heads up, warned him how the operation worked, and Assad has been able to hold it off. That public image of Gaddafi's – it was a put on. The man was no fool. You don't survive for forty years in a place like Libya by being a fool. So Assad, he learned from Gaddafi's mistakes. Plus, Syria isn't as important oil-wise as Libya. Close, but not quite."

Finally Mac interrupted, his mind reeling from Jack's onslaught of information.

"Wait – you haven't said who was really behind Gaddafi's removal. And why?"

Jack nodded, his eyes looking over to both Minnick and Benny, who were both listening intently as well.

"Who is the biggest oil producer in the world Mac?"

Mac answered without hesitation.

"Saudi Arabia."

Jack shook his head.

"Wrong. Not anymore. It's Russia. Saudi Arabia is number two. Studies are showing though that the United States, with all of the new shale explorations, the oil found in the Dakotas, that the United States will be jumping to number one. Now pay attention here Mac – I need you to really let this part sink in.

The Saudis are losing their choke hold on oil production in the world, and that could mean losses of trillions of dollars over the next decade alone. If they can't manipulate the markets like they've been used to doing, they lose money and they lose influence, and most importantly for them - they lose power. Now who was Libya selling its oil to? Russia. That had the Saudis pissed – real pissed. Who is Syria selling its oil to? Russia. And like I said, same thing happening there as went down in Libya. Take it back further. Who was Iraq selling its oil to? Russia. Saudis didn't like it, Saddam told them too fucking bad, and he's taken out - just like Gaddafi. Egypt, same thing.

Algeria, same thing too. They were all pissing off the Saudis and the United Arab Emirates, places like Dubai, who are like the Saudis' little cousins. The two are connected at the hip, the royal families all intermarry with one another."

As Jack continued with his explanation, Mac inhaled sharply at his mentioning of Dubai, the very city Dasha had indicated she preferred to spend most of her time when not in New York or London.

"That's why there's this war on energy production in America right now Mac. This administration has been put in place to do just that, bought and paid for by oil money outside of the United States. That rig that blew up in the gulf – that was no accident. The slow response to clean it up, this administration wanted that bad press. They wanted it to create more momentum for the anti-oil movement in this country. It's an all out war on coal, and oil and natural gas – these people are selling out any hope we have for energy independence because that's what the Saudis need to happen if they are to regain control over the international oil markets. They need control over the Libyan oil, and the Algerian oil, and the Egyptian oil, and any other governments they can topple and replace with people willing to do their bidding. That oil that is now back up and running and going to Great Britain and France and other European nations? Those profits are being directed back to the Saudis Mac – I guarantee it man. When Gaddafi was taken out, it was the Saudis telling the Russians to back the fuck off, and the United States, our government, was right there to help it happen, because it was the Saudis who put this administration into power.

That's why I'm so uneasy about what we are doing going into Libya now. I'm afraid Mac. I'm afraid our job will be to make sure it keeps happening. I'm afraid we aint' working for America on this one. Do you get what I'm saying Mac? Minnick said to us yesterday that it didn't matter where the money we were being paid came from, as long as we were working for the good guys. Well, what if we aren't working for the good guys on this Mac? What if…what if we're the bad guys?"

The drone of the jet's engines gently vibrated the cabin interior as Mac sat silent, looking from Jack, to Minnick, and then to Benny. The others were as quiet regarding Jack's information as Mac was.

Mac found himself wondering if some or even most of what Jack believed could actually be true. If so, how much danger were he and his men actually in while they hunkered down in Libya for the next twenty one days? Jack must have sensed Mac's thoughts, as he leaned forward in his seat again, his face grim.

"This assignment ain't right Mac. I'm telling you, we are being used for something far beyond anything we've been involved with before. I don't know exactly what it is, but I can feel it in my gut man. This is my last assignment Mac. I can't look the other way anymore. I don't trust the people giving us this work. We get out of this one alive…that's it for me. I'm out. I'm done."

Mac looked out his own window, his mind repeating the words Dasha had spoken to him the day before.

My position with the United Nations involves a new approach Mr. Walker. For too long that institution has been viewed as something of a joke among the world's political class. There are those who feel it must…evolve. We must move beyond countless meetings and agendas, and idiotic statements that have no basis in reality, and are ultimately, non-binding. We have been pleased to see this view received rather warmly by the current American administration. Call it a more…pro-active approach. We wish to give the United Nations real teeth, so that the world will come to realize if provoked, it can and more importantly will, bite back.

Think of it as a new beginning for the organization. A…New United Nations, if you will.

VII.

The descent onto the San Vito runway was without incident, Captain Bob expertly handling the Gulfstream's approach and bringing the aircraft to a stop near a long, light red metallic building where a large, silver SUV was parked. Mac was surprised to see the Gulfstream was only one of several aircraft that were coming into and out of the former American military air station, even during the nighttime hours. Several light blue United Nations vans were also busily moving about at the facility.

Captain Bob emerged from the cockpit and opened the exit door for Mac's team. The captain shook each of their hands again, wishing the men luck. He told Mac as soon as the jet was re-fueled, he was returning to D.C. for several weeks of needed downtime.

"Too old for this shit anymore Mac. Got a few more runs left in me and then I'll be hanging it up."

Mac gripped the captain's hand firmly.

"Hope to see you be the one to fly us back out of here in a few weeks Captain."

Mac quickly moved down the Gulfstream's exit steps, spotting who he assumed was the San Vito contact making his way toward them where he had been waiting in the parked SUV which Mac noted had the same United Nations identification markings as the light blue vans did.

"Hello gentleman! My name is Angelo Moretti. I am your facilitator contact here at San Vito. I have been in communication with your Mr. Tilley and understand you are to be given direct transport to Benghazi, Libya immediately."

As soon as he heard Moretti mention Benghazi, Mac found himself glancing over at Jack, who in turn stood silently as he watched the comings and goings of the many United Nations vans as they drove back and forth across the airport.

Angelo was several inches shy of six foot, with a friendly, rounded face and neatly trimmed black mustache. What remained of his hair was carefully combed over his scalp in a failing attempt to hide his balding. As he spoke in a heavy Italian accent, his eyes would flare open while his hands would help to enunciate each of his words.

"Please gentlemen – if you would follow me this way."

As he followed Angelo to the SUV, Mac's hand went instinctively to his sidearm that was holstered on his right hip. Jack, Minnick, and Benny also carried their own handguns.

The temperature inside the SUV was considerably cooler, its AC blasting cold air from the dash vents. Mac sat in the passenger seat opposite Angelo, while the other three were seated behind them.

"Ok, just a short drive to the other end of the runway. You will be taking a humanitarian transport flight into Benina International Airport, which is just ten minutes drive from downtown Benghazi. This aircraft has already made multiple flights into and out of Benina, so it should not illicit any undo notice from the local authorities. The flight crew has been told you are part of a food provisions mission and your identifications, which you will find in the glove box there, fully supports that scenario. You location on the plane will be at the very back, so you should not even be required to speak to the flight crew at all if you so choose. Once we arrive in Benina, I shall drive you personally to Benghazi and your safe house, where further instructions and materials will be made available to you."

Before passing them out to each of his men, Mac scanned the four identification packets that were located in the glove box. They appeared to be of high quality. Over the years, Mac had certainly had to work with much worse.

Angelo parked the SUV next to an older turboprop Antonov An-24 transport craft. Mac was familiar with the Antonov and its relatively slow flying speeds, and estimated the flight to Benghazi would take a little over two and a half hours.

Angelo opened his door and jumped out onto the tarmac.

"Come on then – the flight is scheduled to leave soon."

Mac's voice called out from inside the SUV.

"Angelo! You forgetting something?"

Angelo glanced back at Mac, a frown showing his confusion over the question.

"No…everything is ready."

Mac opened the passenger door and made his way around the SUV as Jack, Benny and Minnick followed close behind him. They already knew what Mac was referring to.

"Tilley said there would be forty thousand waiting for us here. He said you were to be the one to get it to us."

Angelo's wide eyes grew wider as his hands flew to the sides of his round face.

"Oh, of course! Yes! I have it right here!"

The Italian reached into an inner pocket of his light brown blazer and removed a simple white envelope.

"Here you go – forty thousand dollars per my instructions from Mr. Tilley."

Mac's lips tightened as he took the envelope from Angelo and passed it to Minnick.

"Make sure it's all there."

Minnick quickly counted the currency, which was in Euros, and then confirmed to Mac it came to forty thousand.

Angelo smiled back at the four men, his head nodding repeatedly at Minnick's confirmation of the amount.

"See – no problems! Now, everyone, please follow me. They are preparing for takeoff already. We need to go."

Less than three hours later, sitting in the back of the An-24, Mac and the others landed at the Benina airport just outside of Benghazi. Mac's watch indicated it was nearly three in the morning, Benghazi time.

The devil's hour...

VIII.

Mac had the team wait until all of the food supplies had already been unloaded from the plane before leading his men to the tarmac outside. Angelo already had another United Nations' vehicle waiting for them – this one was a simple white minivan.

"Ok gentleman, now I'll take you to the safe house. It's about ten minutes drive from here, so remember that. If you need to get out of Benghazi fast, get to this airport and demand to speak to a man by the name of Louis Danton. He is the ranking U.N. humanitarian official here at Benina. He has my direct contact, so if there's trouble, he can get to me quick and help will be on its way for you. If anyone attempts to prevent you from seeing Mr. Danton, a hundred Euros or so should easily remove that interference.

Do any of you have any questions so far?"

Mac and the others remained silent for a moment until Jack spoke up.

"This Danton, is he French?"

Angelo nodded.

"Yes, though he speaks very good English as well as Arabic."

Jack followed up with another question.

"And do you trust him?"

Again Angelo nodded.

"Of course."

Jack didn't looked convinced, but by then was already stepping into the van.

The streets of Benghazi were oddly quiet. Even at this early hour, Mac thought a Mediterranean port city with well over a half million occupants would have much more activity. He glanced at the passenger seat's rear view mirror and saw the faint outline of headlights some hundred yards behind them. They were being followed. Besides their van and the vehicle behind them, no other cars were on the road.

"Does this van have any weapons Angelo?"

Angelo appeared startled at the question as he shook his head no.

"There are weapons and ammunition at the safe house, as I said earlier."

The vehicle behind them had sped up slightly. Mac turned to look at his men seated behind him.

"Be ready."

Jack, Minnick, and Benny knew that when Mac spoke those two words, he meant it. Each of them quietly removed their handguns from their holsters, their adrenalin already beginning to heighten in preparation of potential trouble.

Mac looked over at Angelo, who continued to appear oblivious to the other vehicle tailing them.

"Angelo, I need you to turn onto a side street please, preferably to make a hard right and then speed up before pulling off to the side of the road. I want you to do it at the next available street…I see one coming up to us now."

Mac's voice was calm, but his team sensed he too was readying himself for battle.

Angelo, looking confused, pointed a finger at the windshield.

"We are not to the safe house yet. Five more minutes."

Mac's hand snapped across the space between he and Angelo and grabbed the steering wheel, sending the van veering onto a narrow side road.

"Give this thing some fucking gas Angelo – NOW!"

Angelo's eyes widened again as he pushed down on the van's accelerator, moving the vehicle quickly past rows of single level residential homes.

"Now stop – and cut the lights!"

The van screeched to a halt, though before it had come to a full stop, Mac was already outside, his P226 at the ready. The residential street was silent but for the scraping of boots over tightly packed gravel as Jack, Benny, and Minnick moved to positions approximately thirty yards from one another, quickly fading into the darkness of the dimly lit street.

Mac stayed by the van, keeping an eye on both the ends of the street, as well as Angelo's movements as he moved out slowly from the driver's seat. In the distance, the barking of a dog carried across the humid Benghazi pre-dawn air.

The silence was suddenly ripped away as a speeding van identical to the one they were riding in with Angelo, approached their location with its headlights turned off. It appeared to be doing at least sixty miles an hour. Mac knew that very soon the van's high beams would be turned on in an attempt to momentarily blind them.

"I need one of you to get yourself behind that incoming. Be ready."

Mac made out the form of Jack moving swiftly down the street, hiding along the way where he could find a tree or shrub to do so. The van was now less than fifty yards away and closing fast.

It was at that moment Mac heard Angelo attempting to sneak behind him. He had been expecting this from the Italian as soon as he noted they were being followed out of the Benina airport. Nobody who was to have been as integral to the assignment as Angelo could have been so oblivious to being tailed. The only question in Mac's mind now was if he would keep Angelo alive, or simply kill him dead now.

"Angelo, don't make the mistake of underestimating me. Anyone who has done that, finds themselves leaving this earth soon after."

As predicted, the approaching van turned on its headlights. That was Mac's cue to hit the ground, rolling almost too fast for the eye to follow as Angelo strained to see what was in front of him. Mac fired a single round into Angelo's right wrist, causing the Italian to drop his gun and cry out in shock and pain. Mac was already up and running to the back of their van as the other van's occupants began firing in his direction. Soon their gunfire was met with return fire from each side of the street as Minnick and Benny emerged from the shadows then almost immediately followed by Jack squeezing several rounds off from behind. It took Mac's team no more than ten seconds to kill the five men from the other van.

Walking back to the side of their own van, Mac saw Angelo's body crumpled against the rear tire, his chest heaving for air. Given the blood soaking through the front of his shirt, it appeared he had taken a bullet from one of the men firing from one of the other vans. Mac leaned down and looked Angelo in the eyes before delivering a hard slap across the man's face.

"I need you to focus Angelo, ok? Who did you make this deal with?"

Angelo's stared back at Mac, his face expressing the shock over the realization he was dying.

"Angelo – who are you working for?"

The Italian found a fragment of whatever courage he may have once lived his life with, raising his head from his chest and sneering back at Mac as he spit out a response in Arabic.

"Fuck you American pig. There's nothing you'll do to change any of this...it's already done. We win – you lose."

Angelo's last breath was cut short as his lungs filled with his own blood, and a gurgling rasp wheezed from his throat as his body slumped to the side and onto the street.

Mac stood up as his mind raced to assess the situation. The safe house was not an option – Angelo clearly had no intention of taking them to any such place, and besides, they had no idea where it was. Angelos's final words were spoken in perfect Arabic, though the accent was not Libyan. Mac had spent years learning that language, and had worked throughout the Middle East. The accent was unmistakably Turkish, which though somewhat similar to Arabic, was its own language. What that meant as far as who Angelo may have been associated with, Mac had no idea and at present, it didn't really matter. His job now was to relocate and keep his men as safe as possible until further options presented themselves.

"Benny, Minnick, check the bodies. Look for any identification – and be quick."

It took no more than a minute for Minnick to report back.

"Nothing Mac. The van is the same as ours, but there's nothing in it, and no identification on any of the bodies. I took their weapons. They were all carrying brand new, matching Makarovs. What are a bunch of Libyan thugs doing carrying Russian handguns Mac?"

Mac didn't know, and at that point, he didn't care. His job was to get him and his men the hell off this street.

"In the van – let's go."

The other three in Mac's team followed the order without speaking. Like Mac, they too already fully understood how dire the situation already was, and the fact that in their immediate future, it was likely to get much worse.

As he drove slowly back onto the main road, Mac could hear Jack's sarcastic remark from behind the driver's seat.

"Are we enjoying our stay in Benghazi yet?"

Mac ignored Jack's words, his mind struggling to come up with a viable plan, though each time he returned to a question that remained blaring back at him, its implications chilling the former Navy SEAL to his core.

Can I trust Tilley – or was he part of this? And if he was, then why?

Without Tilley's help, his team's chances for getting out of Benghazi alive were greatly diminished. Tilley was the one who lined up Angelo, but that didn't mean Tilley was involved in whatever Angelo was. He could be though.

"Shit."

Mac didn't intend to say the word out loud, but after he did, Minnick, who sat in the passenger seat, nodded in response.

"Yeah – shit. That about sums it up doesn't it? And you're probably thinking the same thing I am, aren't you? Can we trust Tilley to help bail us out of this mess, or was he part of it?"

Benny leaned forward, his head emerging from the darkness of the van's back seat.

"Bullshit. Tilley had nothing to do with this. I heard that Angelo speaking to Mac in Arabic. He wasn't Italian, or if he was, he was a Muslim first. Tilley got burned by whoever Angelo really is the same as we did. We can't afford to be throwing the baby out with the bathwater Mac."

Mac was heading back to the Benina airport. With all of the matching U.N. vans located there, they would be able to blend in enough to buy them just a little more time – enough time for him to decide whether or not to risk reaching out to Tilley for help.

The airport security remained as non-existent as when they had left it. Mac simply drove past the gates and into the primary facility area, parking the van next to a row of three other identical vans.

"What do you think Jack? Do I give Tilley a call?"

Jack remained motionless in the back seat, his eyes closed as he focused on his breathing as Mac waited patiently for a response. Finally Jack opened his eyes and offered a thin smile back at Mac.

"We don't have much choice at this point Mac. The way I see it, either you call him, or I will. He's our best shot right now of getting out of this shithole."

Mac didn't take Jack's words as a sign of disrespect. In fact, they were just the opposite. They cleared Mac's head of options, and made the decision a simple one – he had no choice but to reach out to Tilley. Mac took out his cell and dialed Tilley's direct contact number, the one used only for assignment emergencies.

Tilley picked up the call on the second ring.

"What's wrong? This seems early for a check in."

Mac paused as he considered his words carefully.

"We've been compromised. The Italian contact was bad. No safe house available."

Now it was Tilley's turn to pause. Mac waited him out, staying silent as well.

"Any casualties?"

"Affirmative – but the team is fine."

Mac could sense Tilley's indecision over the phone.

"Ok…give me thirty minutes. Hold on and call me again in thirty minutes."

Tilley hung up, leaving Mac to wonder what Tilley could come up with in thirty minutes that would bail his team out of a situation thousands of miles away in Benghazi, Libya.

"What did he say Mac?"

Mac looked over at Minnick, who was calmly cleaning his glasses as he asked the question.

"He said he wanted me to call him back in thirty minutes."

Minnick's brow furrowed as he considered Mac's words.

"Why have us wait thirty minutes? Why doesn't he call as soon as he has an option in place for us?"

Minnick said what Mac had been thinking. Tilley's response felt like a stall. Mac had intentionally avoided telling him their current location. Tilley was smart though, smart enough to guess that Mac would return their van to the location that offered them the most cover – the airport.

Mac's eyes scanned the vehicles around them. A plane similar to the one they had arrived in was preparing for take off no more than a hundred yards from where they were parked. In just a couple more hours, the place would be crawling with people as the day's business was fully underway. The bodies of the five men and Angelo had likely already been discovered. The van that had been left in the street was the same one they were sitting in now. They were common to this airport. That meant it would be the first place the authorities would go looking.

They needed to move.

"Ok, you three stay put. I'm gonna find us different transportation."

Mac left the van, walking between vehicles as he searched for one that would allow them to drive into the main part of the city undetected, something without a United Nations badge on it. Some three hundred feet inside the airport's main entrance, Mac spotted four empty taxis parked alongside a row of white single wide trailers. The vehicles were basic black four door sedans with the words "Benghazi Comfort Taxi" prominently displayed on each side. Mac figured if there were already four of the taxis parked here this early in the morning, the city streets would be teeming with them within the hour.

The first taxi was locked, as was the second. The driver's door of the third taxi opened and Mac spotted a single key hanging from the ignition.

Bingo.

The car started easily, though Mac could smell the body odor of its regularly assigned driver. Whoever it was, they needed to invest in a hell of a lot more deodorant. Pulling the car away from the other three, Mac drove it slowly toward the parked United Nations van where his team waited.

He left the car running as he stepped back outside and motioned for Jack, Benny, and Minnick to get into the taxi. Mac's eyes scanned the area to see if anyone had noticed them. The airport remained relatively quiet even as Mac spotted what appeared to be an approaching passenger jet approaching from the skies.

"Ok – let's go."

The taxi left the airport without incident and within minutes Mac was driving around a massive roundabout, his taxi one of more than a dozen matching vehicles doing the same. Mac's phone rang – it was Tilley. He hadn't waited for Mac to call after all.

"Are you on the move?"

Mac considered the question, then lied.

"No - the airport."

"Ok…listen carefully. Hadaik – Area Fifteen. Villa Four. Only one of you enters. Ask to speak to Ella. We're still operational. Do you understand? We're ok. Ella will take you to where you need to go. Call to confirm when you get there."

Tilley hung up, leaving Mac to ponder if he should follow the instructions and drive to the address given.

"He wants us to head out to Hadaik, Area Fifteen, Villa Four. Meet a woman named Ella. Says we're still operational. Give me some feedback boys. What do you think?"

Minnick, sitting in the passenger seat, was the first to respond to Mac.

"We do it. I thought about what Jack and Benny said. Until we know for sure otherwise, we have to trust Tilley Mac."

Mac punched in the address given to him by Tilley into the taxi's dashboard GPS. They were seven miles from the location. Outside, the streets of Benghazi were quickly becoming increasingly congested. Seven miles in this traffic was going to take some time.

"Three cars back. Black SUV."

Mac's eyes looked in his rear view mirror, following Benny's description. A large, American-made SUV was in fact three cars behind them, its darkened windows making it impossible to see its occupants.

The taxi shot forward, passing several cars on the right side as Mac pushed down hard on its accelerator while watching to see how the SUV would react.

"Definitely following us Mac."

The SUV moved quickly to the left side of the road, coming within inches of hitting several other vehicles as it neared their taxi. Whoever was driving it was well trained.

Mac moved the taxi back to the center lane and slowed down again, trying to keep at least one other vehicle between them and the SUV. The GPS indicated they were still six miles from the address Tilley had given them.

"To hell with this."

Mac mashed the taxi's accelerator all the way to the floor, swerving between several other vehicles before veering off onto a side street. The car's engine howled in protest as its speedometer indicated nearly eighty miles an hour.

"Still there Mac - hundred yards and closing."

Both Benny and Jack had drawn their handguns as they looked out the taxi's back window.

Mac kept the accelerator to the floor as they approached nearly a hundred miles an hour.

"Hold on."

The taxi's tires screamed against the pavement as Mac pulled the wheel hard to the left and onto another side street, barely missing a row of parked vehicles and causing Mac to almost lose control as he frantically pulled the taxi back toward the center of the street.

Jack's Alabama drawl called out from the back seat.

"Hey! Keep it on the road badass."

Mac responded to Jack's quip by raising his right middle finger as his foot again slammed down on the accelerator.

"On your right Mac, forty yards - dumpsters."

Mac saw where Minnick was pointing to. A row of ten or so large green metallic dumpsters. The SUV could no longer be seen directly behind them as Mac pulled the taxi directly behind the dumpsters and slammed on the brakes, bringing the car to a sudden stop.

Only a few seconds passed before the SUV was spotted driving slowly down the street Mac had just pulled off of. As the SUV began to pass the dumpsters, Mac put the taxi in reverse and inched the car backwards, always keeping the dumpsters between them and the SUV's line of sight until the SUV had finally passed them completely as it continued heading down the street.

"Nice driving Louisiana."

Mac chuckled at Jack's compliment.

"Thanks Alabama."

IX.

Mac waited another few minutes to make certain the SUV didn't return, and then proceeded to drive back onto the main roadway and toward the address Tilley had instructed them to arrive at. Ten minutes later, they arrived at a squat white building with a single palm tree that loomed over the right side of the aging structure. A sign hung over the door that read, "Libyan Media Freedom Network". An older, tan Mercedes 300 was the only vehicle parked in front of the building.

Minnick pointed toward the palm tree.

"They have a security camera just to the left of the tree, half inch security bars across the two windows, and the door looks to be a newer Ceco model. Whatever this place is, they've taken precautions to protect the people inside."

Mac parked the taxi in an alley about three hundred feet away from the tan Mercedes. That way if the SUV that had been following them found it, their location inside the Libyan Media Freedom Network building would be difficult to determine. There were at least another seven buildings within similar distance from the parked taxi.

"I need you three to set up a perimeter shield, nearest one to be no more than sixty feet from the entrance. Want one of you within eyesight of this location here. If that SUV comes back and checks out the taxi, I want to know who we are dealing with – are they Libyans, CIA, whatever."

Jack offered to remain near the taxi, while Benny and Minnick took locations nearer the parked Mercedes as Mac began to walk toward the building's entrance. He paused to allow the security camera plenty of time to see him before pushing a small white intercom button housed just to the left of the door. Minnick had been right – it was an almost brand new Ceco security door.

"I'm here to see Ella."

A short buzzing sound emitted from the top of the door frame, indicating Mac could now pull the door open. Just inside the door was a small six by six room where another door matching the one outside was located directly in front of where Mac stood. Another security camera was housed in the upper right corner of the small room.

"Who sent you?"

The voice came from a small intercom placed in the low ceiling just above Mac's head.

"Tilley."

The second door opened, leading to a surprisingly well lit and expensively furnished waiting area. Two armed men dressed in matching black dress shirts and khakis stood approximately six feet apart from each other looking back at Mac. They each carried X95 assault rifles, perhaps the most common weapon of choice for Israeli Special Forces. It was a weapon that carried light, but still packed a serious punch, allowing fully automatic, thirty two round capabilities.

Each of the men was slightly taller than Mac, and at least ten years younger. Their dark eyes regarded Mac without emotion, a sign of a well trained soldier.

Mac heard heeled steps approaching from a hallway that opened up from the back left of the room from which emerged a blonde woman of medium height and athletic build. She appeared to be no more than forty years of age, with a somewhat long and narrow face, full lips, and wide, dark eyes that sat under high arching brows. Her hair fell casually over her shoulders as she stopped to look at Mac.

"Mr. Walker?"

She spoke his real name, proving to Mac she was in fact in contact with Tilley. Mac nodded his head once back at her.

"Please follow me Mr. Walker."

The woman turned and walked back down the hallway from which she had emerged, her steps quick and confident, requiring Mac to move swiftly to catch up. She opened the second door they passed on the right side of the hallway and entered what appeared to be a conference room. It contained a long black metallic desk with a glass top, and several matching black chairs. Unlike the reception area, no other furnishings were in the room, and no artwork hung from the walls.

"Take a seat Mr. Walker."

Mac sat on one side of the table as the woman took a seat opposite him.

"Do you know who I am?"

Mac shook his head.

"No idea – just following the directions Tilley gave me. Care to say how much you know about me?"

The woman's mouth curled into a slight smile. Though her features were somewhat hard, Mac found her attractive in a she-can-kick-the-shit-out-of-somebody kind of way.

"I know almost as little about you as you do me, Mr. Walker. What I do know is that you are in a bit of difficulty since arriving in Benghazi. I also know that I owe your Mr. Tilley a favor. This help I am now providing you is payment for that debt."

Mac finally placed her accent – like the weapons in the reception room, she was Israeli.

"Whatever help you can provide is appreciated. Right now, we still don't have any real idea what the hell we're doing here."

"As you were told, my name is Ella. This building you now sit in is a media center…of sorts."

Mac smiled.

"Of course…of sorts."

"We will provide you transport to your safe house Mr. Walker. What you find there, I cannot tell you. Once that transport has been completed, I ask that you not return here. Our business, such that it is, will have been completed. Do you understand?"

The door to the conference room opened, followed by one of the two armed men from the reception room stepping inside. Though the man's voice remained calm and measured, Mac noted his eyes betrayed concern.

"Two vehicles outside Ella. Black SUVs. They appear to be securing the perimeter."

Ella's eyes burned into Mac.

"You were followed?"

Mac nodded.

"Yeah – thought we had lost them though."

Ella tilted her head to the side as her eyebrows raised.

"It appears you didn't do such a good job of that Mr. Walker. Do you have men outside?"

Mac glanced at the armed man and then looked back at Ella.

"Three. They're armed with handguns."

Ella leaned over the table, her voice coming out in a seething whisper.

"And are you better with a gun than you are at not attracting attention and leading trouble right to our door Mr. Walker?"

Mac's eyes flashed indignation as he met Ella's stare.

"I'd say I'm better than fair if it comes to that."

Ella offered a cold smile in return.

"Well then, let's see…if it comes to that."

Ella rose from her chair and walked quickly toward a narrow door near the back left corner of the conference room. She opened it up and withdrew another of the X95 assault rifles and threw it to Mac.

"Mr. Walker, this is Udi. You will be accompanying him to the roof. You are to follow his lead Mr. Walker, not the other way around – do you understand?"

Mac looked at the armed man and then nodded back to Ella.

"Hey, your house – your rules. What are you doing?"

Ella calmly pulled her hair back into a pony tail and straightened her black blouse and matching skirt.

"I am going outside to see what these assholes want."

Mac's mouth dropped open in shock as he watched Ella make her way down the hall and back outside as Udi motioned for Mac to follow him further down the hallway which led to a narrow stairwell with steps leading up.

A few seconds later both Mac and Udi were lying atop the flat roof on their stomachs looking down at the two black SUVs as Ella approached three men who stood just outside the building's entrance. Mac scanned the area for any sign of his men, but wherever they were, they remained hidden.

As Ella approached the three men, four more emerged from the SUVs, two of them armed with assault rifles. All of the men were casually dressed, and all appeared to be white. Mac's eyes strained to make out the face of the man Ella was speaking with, a short, balding man who was familiar to him.

Densmore. Mark Densmore.

Mark Densmore was FBI. Mac had crossed paths with him almost ten years ago when Mac was still doing Project Icon work out of the Department of Defense.

What the hell is FBI doing in Benghazi?

Maybe Densmore had transferred over to CIA or NSA. That kind of transfer wasn't common, but it did happen.

"Company."

Udi had spotted a large military transport truck carrying what appeared to be at least twenty armed Libyan militia approaching the SUVs. Densmore's men noticed the truck soon after Udi did, and moved quickly to the other side of their SUVs.

"Get Ella back inside. Now!"

Udi had spoken into a small handheld communicator to the other armed Israeli man who stood just inside the building entrance. One of Densmore's men grabbed Ella's right arm and was attempting to push her toward one of their vehicles. Mac watched in admiration as Ella's left palm smoothly smashed into the lower part of the man's nose, sending him reeling backward. The other armed Israeli who Udi had just communicated with, reached Ella and placed himself between her and the SUVs.

Mac counted up Densmore's men – they totaled seven. Two were armed with assault rifles, the remaining five were holding handguns. The military transport truck now sat twenty yards from the SUVs as its occupants jumped out onto the ground. Mac quickly counted twenty three of them – all carrying assault rifles. Their behavior, the way they walked so casually toward Densmore's men, indicated the Libyan militants were not well trained, as was so often the case in this part of the world. They may have had numbers, but they knew fuck-all about tactics.

Interestingly, Ella stood her own ground as she began to yell out in Arabic at the approaching militants.

"We want no trouble here! These men were just about to leave. They were simply asking a few questions."

One of the taller militants, a very thin and haggard looking older man began to approach Ella, but was stopped by the Israeli's X95 pointing directly at him. The militant, armed with what Mac believed to be an older model AK-47, lifted his weapon to the side with his right hand while holding up his left hand palm forward.

"We are not here about you. Your news articles are of no interest to us. But these Americans, hiding like dogs, driving around our city, stirring up trouble, thinking they are above our laws, we have no use for them. Come out from behind your cars coward Americans. Come out so that we can see your faces."

Ella stepped toward the older militant leader with both of her hands held up in front of her.

"Nobody wants any trouble here. Hasn't Libya seen enough of that kind of trouble? These men were just leaving, and I think it would be a very good idea if you and your men did the same."

"What does the Jewish bitch know about Libya's troubles? Go back to Jew hell bitch!"

The comment was shouted by a large, heavy set militant with a massive dark beard and an unruly head of black and grey hair. Mac noted murmuring from other militia – they had not known that Ella was Israeli.

"Kill the Jewish pig bitch! Cut out her tongue for thinking she can tell Muslim men what to do!"

Several of the Libyans cheered the comment. Mac sensed the situation was reaching critical. He saw several other vehicles slowing down as their drivers leaned out to see what was going on. Within minutes, they would be dealing with much more than the twenty odd armed militia members – they could have an enraged Muslim mob on their hands.

Ella, also sensing the heightened danger she was now in, began to back slowly toward the building's entrance.

"Where are you going Jew bitch?"

Mac watched as Densmore and two of his men cut off Ella's path back to the building. Udi was now pointing his gun into Densmore's back.

"Easy there – we ain't quite at the point of no return just yet."

Udi glared back at Mac as he continued to point his weapon at Densmore.

"I don't take orders from you. You're supposed to follow my lead – remember?"

The older Libyan who had first spoken to Ella turned around, trying to calm his men.

"We are not here for bloodshed. We are here to tell the Americans to get out of our country. To go back home and leave Libya to Libyans."

"Fuck the Americans and fuck the Jews!"

Others among the Libyans began to repeat the words.

"Fuck the Americans and fuck the Jews!"

Densmore finally appeared to realize he was in just as much danger as Ella and her men were, as he trotted back behind one of the SUV's, yelling into a cell phone that he needed help. Mac wondered who the FBI agent was talking to.

Several more Libyans had stopped their cars and were now walking toward the military transport truck, some of them already repeating the newly introduced mantra.

"Fuck the Americans and fuck the Jews!"

Mac spotted Jack moving slowly behind a row of palm trees as the sound of approaching sirens could be heard in the distance while Densmore and his men quickly jumped back into their vehicles and began to slowly drive away, leaving the growing and increasingly angry mob of Libyans to gather in front of Ella's building. The bearded militant who had first shouted out that Ella was Jewish, pointed his assault rifle into the air and fired off several rounds. Several others among the armed Libyans were soon doing the same.

Mac knew it would not be long before one of them pointed a weapon and fired it at the building itself.

The sound of the sirens grew closer as a Benghazi police car pulled in behind the gathering mob. A few of the militia members approached the police officer, firing their guns into the air while screaming for him to leave them alone. Mac watched as the police car quickly backed up and drove away.

So much for the cowardly cavalry...

Udi put his communicator to his ear, listening as he was told Ella was back inside the building.

As many as seventy Libyans were now gathered at the building entrance.

"Kill the Americans and kill the Jews!"

Mac looked over at Udi and winked.

"Hey, the good news is they changed their minds about fucking us!"

Ella approached from behind both Mac and Udi as they continued to lie on their stomachs peeking out at the Libyans below.

"So very glad you were sent to me Mr. Walker. I just love dealing with this kind of trouble so early in the day. You know, life's just so boringly simple when you're a Jewish woman in the middle of a city run by Muslim men who are born to hate everything about you."

Mac looked back to reply to Ella's words, but paused as he watched her moving forward along the roof, crouched low and carrying in both hands a World War Two era MG-42 machine gun.

"Udi, after I get this set up, I want you to yell out to those assholes down there that we mean business. If they don't disperse, we are going to cut them into ribbons."

Udi smiled back at Ella as she expertly extended the doubled legged base of the MG-42 and positioned its barrel to point just above the heads of the Libyans below.

"Mr. Walker, you can make yourself useful by helping to feed the ammo. That is, if you know how to do that."

Mac grabbed onto the ammo belt.

"Oh, I think I can manage."

Udi stood up and looked down at the Libyans gathered in front of the building and shouted down to them in Arabic.

"Hey! Hey! We are going to ask you to leave this area now! If you fail to do so, we are prepared to defend ourselves. We are well armed. Do you understand?"

"Send out the Jew bitch!"

The Libyans cheered the suggestion as they fired more rounds into the air.

Ella's jaw clamped down as she moved the MG-42's barrel several more inches higher to ensure she wouldn't hit anyone below or away from the building. Mac knew the gun was rated to fire at a thousand yards.

The sound of the MG-42 in action was similar to that of an incredibly loud and violent chain saw. Within a few seconds Ella had unleashed a barrage of over sixty rounds, the results of which were instantaneous.

Bellow them, the Libyans scattered, their eyes wide in terror of the death that could rain down from above. Again Ella pulled the trigger, and again the MG-42 snarled its menacing warning.

A mere minute later and no sign of the gathering Libyan mob remained. They were a people well versed in the sound of a deadly weapon, and knew when it was time to move and move fast.

Ella stood up and brushed off the dust from the front of her skirt and blouse and then looked back down at Mac.

"Ok then Mr. Walker, I guess it's time to get you to that safe house of yours. Please meet me downstairs as soon as possible."

Mac watched the back of Ella as she made her way across the rooftop, not aware of the wide smile that crossed his face – that is until Udi's fist punched him in the shoulder.

"Not for you to look at Mr. Walker."

Mac looked back at Udi, the smile still on his face.

"Are all Israeli women like that?"

Udi's face was again expressionless as he stood up.

"It is often said Mr. Walker, that it is not the Israeli men the Muslim radicals should fear, but rather our women. That said, Ella is something…special. That can be both a good thing, and a bad thing. You would do well to know that. She is not to be trifled with Mr. Walker."

Mac looked down to see Jack staring back up at him from the ground, his head shaking from side to side.

"Told you Mac – fucking Benghazi."

Mac looked out across the city streets, thinking he could just catch a glimpse of the blue watered Mediterranean Sea. The temperature already felt to be nearing ninety. They had been in Benghazi for less than twelve hours.

X.

…Mac's phone rang. It was Tilley.

Mac hesitated answering, still uncertain whether the man could be trusted. By the fourth ring he decided to hear what Tilley had to say.

"Mac – you there? I was able to get a hold of someone I know in State who has been hunkered down in Benghazi for the last few months. They said they would send out someone to help you get settled in over there. Have they arrived at Ella's location yet?"

Again Mac found himself trying to quickly process the information Tilley was giving him. Tilley must have been referring to Densmore who, the last time Mac checked, was FBI, not State Department.

"I saw a guy named Mark Densmore and a few other men show up here. I know of Densmore – he's FBI. Or he was. Is that who you're talking about?"

Tilley went silent, and Mac knew he had just surprised him with his knowledge of Densmore's FBI connection, and was likely also shocked that Mac had spoken the name over the phone. Good, if Tilley was lying to him, Mac had to rattle the other man to improve his chances of catching him in a lie.

"Did you say FBI, Mac? That this Densmore is…FBI?"

"That's right – we ran in the same circles about ten years ago. I don't know the man well, but I do know him."

Mac could hear Tilley clearing his throat, a sign he was considering what he had just been told. Perhaps Tilley was as surprised to learn of FBI being in Benghazi as Mac was.

'You sound surprised Tilley, and given you're supposed to be the one who brought my team this assignment, that don't sit real well with me, you know? We just sent home one pissed off mob of Muslims here, and I'm sure they'll be back as soon as they clean the shit from their pants, so how about you tell me straight up what the fuck is going on? Why the hell do we have FBI in Benghazi?"

Tilley's reply came back slow – he was being very careful of the words he used.

"Mac, I know I have to be looking pretty suspicious to you right now. I get it, and at this point, all I can do is apologize and do my best for you to keep the assignment proceeding so you stay safe and eventually we all get paid. I have no idea on the FBI information…if you saw who you say you saw, then the first thing I'm going to do after talking to you is confirm that information here on my end. My contact is with the State Department – at least officially. That is who was supposed to send you some help out there. And I trust him one hundred percent Mac. I really do. I know at this point you don't trust me, and that's ok, but hopefully after Ella gets you set up, I'll start to earn that trust back."

Mac sensed Tilley was being sincere, though he also had to consider the man was likely at this point in his career, an exceptionally proficient liar.

"Who is this Ella? How do you know her?"

Tilley's tone was slightly more relaxed.

"Ella Lerner is top tier Mac. That's all I want to say over the phone. You're in very good hands. She owed me one, and her helping you and your team out is payment for that debt. She's nobody you want to fuck with though, so don't even think about it."

Mac grunted, remembering Ella's recent display with the MG-42 machine gun.

"Yeah – saw a bit of that already. She's not so bad on the eyes too."

Tilley chuckled. He was becoming more relaxed – more like his usual self.

"I need you to stay focused Mac. Plus, word is, you already had a bit of down time with a certain attractive and very wealthy someone right before you flew out of D.C. I figure you should have that kind of thing out of your system for at least a few days, right? Just let Ella get you to the safe house and then we can confirm your assignment details once you're settled in."

Mac saw Udi motioning for him to follow him down from the roof and back into the building's interior.

"Ok Tilley – I'll let you know when we are at the safe house."

Mac hung up the cell phone and nodded back to Udi while also noting the street below remained clear of trouble. The angry mob may return soon, but it hadn't done so just yet.

Standing back inside the lobby of the Libyan Freedom Network building, Mac was glad to see the three other members of his crew were already inside and waiting for further instructions. Benny and Minnick appeared calm, though focused, while Jack looked somewhat more on edge.

Ella stood looking back at Mac, her arms crossed over the front of her black blouse.

"I am certain I made clear you were to make your way back down here as soon as possible Mr. Walker. You have kept me waiting."

Mac was about to respond with one of his more typical smart-ass comments, but looking back at Ella's humorless, dark eyes, thought better of it. She was in no mood.

"I apologize – I was speaking with Tilley."

Ella Lerner's mouth curled into a smirk, her high cheekbones made more prominent by having left her blonde hair still pulled back in a pony tail.

"I would imagine your confidence in your Mr. Tilley is a bit…lessened, yes?"

Mac shrugged, looking back at his men to let them know they were in no immediate danger.

"Things went to shit. It happens."

Ella shook her head.

"Not when I'm in charge they don't. I have been told the location of your safe house Mr. Walker. Udi here will see that you are safely transported to there in my vehicle. After that, I must reiterate, our business together is to be concluded. You are not to contact me again. Do you understand?"

Mac simply nodded, though as he looked Ella over again, quietly hoped they would have an opportunity to get to know each other better, and soon.

Unknown to Mac, Ella was hoping the same.

XI.

Mac, Benny, Minnick, and Jack sat inside the tan Mercedes 300 that was parked in the front of Ella's building. Though older, the car's tan leather interior remained in almost new condition, and when Udi turned the ignition, the engine started instantly and idled smoothly.

Mac sat in the front passenger seat while the other three men in his crew sat shoulder to shoulder in the backseat. Udi backed the vehicle slowly onto the street and pulled away smoothly, steadily increasing the Mercedes' speed as he exited off a gravel covered secondary road to turn onto one of Benghazi's primary highways that led to one of the many large suburban areas on the outer portions of Benghazi. Udi expertly moved the Mercedes into and out of traffic as he kept the vehicle's speed above seventy miles an hour.

"Your safe house is located in a residential area just outside the city proper. Very nice neighborhood actually, home to some of the area's wealthier residents. I was told the property is fully gated, and should provide ample security for you."

Mac glanced over at Udi, admiring the Israeli man's driving skills. Udi exited the main road and was once again on a secondary road. Though still somewhat paved, it was covered under a fine layer of desert sand. The Mercedes vaulted forward, now speeding along at nearly ninety miles an hour, causing a large plume of dust to billow up behind them.

Just as Udi described, the properties to the right and left of them were expansive, with large, soft colored stucco buildings and meticulously cared for gardens. While Benghazi had many slums within the city, the homes ringing its borders indicated residents of considerable wealth.

Udi slowed the vehicle and turned sharply left onto a narrow drive that led to a substantial dark ironed gate with two guard towers one each side. The gate was open, allowing Udi to speed through it and travel another hundred yards to the property's main house – an expansive two story structure painted tan and white with massive floor to ceiling windows on the first floor, and several large balconies that jutted out from the second floor. Mac estimated the home to be at least six thousand square feet.

"Here we are gentleman, your safe house, courtesy of your friend Mr. Tilley. My job is done – this is where we part ways. Please follow Ella's instructions – do not contact us again."

Mac, Benny, Minnick and Jack exited the Mercedes and watched as Udi sped off down the long drive and back onto the road, soon to be lost amidst another plume of sand dust that marked his swift departure.

Minnick peered up at the large home and then glanced at Mac.

"Home sweet home, huh?"

Mac ignored the comment, already attempting to call Tilley. The phone rang three times and then went to Tilley's voice mail.

"Tilley – Mac. We've arrived. Awaiting instructions."

Benny began walking toward the home's large, wooden, double-door entrance.

"Might as well check it out while we're waiting to hear back from Tilley."

Mac noted Jack surveying the surroundings. Two other properties were easily in view from where they stood. One to the east of the safe house sat some four hundred yards away, while the other across the street, was likely no more than a few hundred yards. Like the safe house, the other properties appeared to be upper class residences as well.

"Feel like we're too much in the open out here Mac. Don't like it."

Mac's eyes squinted into the increasingly warm and bright Benghazi sun. He understood Jack's concern – he didn't like the location either. While it allowed them to see who was coming, it also made them a much easier target, and given the relative distance from the main city, help would be a long time coming. This particular safe house did seem an odd choice, if for nothing more than it would require them to drive considerable distance to get anywhere.

That said, it was one hell of a nice property.

Benny called out behind him as his hand reached out to push against the entrance door.

"C'mon, let's go inside."

Mac's phone rang, causing Benny and the others to pause and look back at Mac.

"Yeah Tilley, go ahead."

"Are you at the assigned location?"

Mac looked back at the large home's entrance.

"Yeah – that's what I said in my message. We're here. Nice place Tilley, so how about telling us what the hell we're supposed to be doing?"

"Go inside Mac. Check out the home's interior, including the upstairs. Then call me back."

Tilley was keeping the call brief in case there were attempts to intercept their communications. He had already hung up.

Mac saw Jack staring back at him, his face indicating he wanted to know what Tilley had said.

"He didn't say much – just that we should go inside and check it out and then I'm to call him back."

Minnick pointed up into the searing blue Benghazi sky.

"Hey – check it out. That one of ours?"

Mac's eyes followed to where Minnick was pointing, spotting the single military drone that was slowly approaching the vicinity of their safe house, its gray metallic exterior flashing against the sun's rays. The drone's presence gave Mac a slight chill, leaving him with the distinct feeling he was somehow glimpsing a darker future, a time to come when the drone technology of today would be the nightmare of tomorrow.

Minnick's voice cut through Mac's thoughts.

"You ok Mac?"

Mac shook himself from his prognostications, though his eyes still glanced back at the approaching drone.

"Yeah, I'm fine. Something about those drones though…they just don't seem right to me. The way they creep across the sky like that."

Benny was watching the drone intently as well before shrugging and waiving a dismissive hand at it.

"Those drones have saved a lot of lives Mac. They go in so our boys don't have to, and that's all right by me."

Jack shook his head at Benny's words.

"I'd call that short term gain for what could be a whole lot of long-term pain Benny. I'm with Mac – those goddamn drones give me the creeps."

Mac pushed open the large, solid wood entrance door to the safe house.

"C'mon, let's get inside before that thing is on top of us."

The home's interior, though large and expansive, was devoid of almost any furnishings. The lower floor was dominated by a massive great room that included the tiled entrance. The living area was a step down space that housed a massive red stone fireplace. The back half of the first floor had a large kitchen and eating area. Though the home was mostly unfurnished, the kitchen was thankfully well stocked with food and drink, and offered an impressive array of commercial grade stainless appliances. Large, double French doors opened from the back portion of the kitchen into an adjoining courtyard outside of the rear portion of the property. Mac was happy to note how the large back garden was fully fenced by an eight foot high and one foot thick stucco wall, giving the space a reasonable amount of security.

Jack and Minnick were already making their way upstairs via the massive stone and dark stained wood staircase as Mac and Benny followed close behind. The top of the staircase brought them to a large hallway that ran along both sides of the upper floor, ending in simple, three by three square windows at either end of the hall.

Minnick was the first to enter one of the four spacious, top floor bedrooms. Inside he found the only furnishings to be a single bed, small side table and a single lamp. The room had the entrance door and three other doors. One door led to an adjoining bathroom, another door led to a sizeable walk in closet, and the last door led to the outside balcony.

"Hey Mac, check this out."

Just outside the room's balcony, hanging from the wall, was a pair of military grade, night vision capable binoculars. Mac picked the binoculars up and looked them over carefully. They were newer technology to be sure, though contained no markings. He placed them up to his eyes and looked out at the property across the road from them that was now easily in sight from the upper floor of the safe house.

"Son-of-a-bitch!"

Mac was amazed at the distance and clarity capabilities of the binoculars, finding he could make out nearly every detail of that other home's exterior, though the home was hundreds of yards away.

"These are some amazing binoculars. Guessing Tilley had them left here for us."

A quick inspection of the other three upstairs rooms found them identical to the first – with the same pair of binoculars hanging outside of each room's balcony. It was then Mac noted each of the four bedrooms had at least a partial view of the property across the road from the safe house.

"So it looks like we're supposed to sit up here and keep an eye one whoever that is living in the house across the street, huh?"

Minnick's words were exactly what Mac was thinking.

"Yeah – looks that way. I'm gonna call Tilley again."

Minnick stepped onto the balcony and pointed out toward the property they believed they were to be watching.

"Hey Mac – there's company over there."

Without the binoculars, Mac could just make out the shape of a black SUV making its way past what appeared to be a possible guardhouse that was located on the right side of the gated entrance. Placing the binoculars to his eyes, Mac was able to clearly see a Department of State emblem on the SUV's door panel, as well as at least one armed Libyan guard nod to the vehicle as it drove past. As he raised the binoculars up to follow the vehicle's path while it drove into the property compound, Mac was also able to identify the barbed wire that rang the upper portion of the property's wall.

"They have the place ringed in barbed wire, with at least one armed guard at the gate. The guard looks to be Libyan. That's a State Department vehicle that just went inside. Now what the hell is the State Department doing outside Benghazi, and why would they be using Libyan security?"

Benny and Jack had joined Mac and Minnick on the balcony as Mac continued to peer through the binoculars at the increasingly mysterious property across the road.

"Any word on a diplomatic consulate in Benghazi Mac?"

Mac lowered the binoculars and looked back at Minnick. It was a good question, though one he didn't have the faintest clue as to an answer. Before Mac could reply, Jack broke in with his own comment.

"If that property over there is supposed to be an American diplomatic station, why so far from the main city? Why so far from local authorities? And why would they be using Libyans to guard the entrance? Suppose it could be a private security contract, but in a place this dangerous? Why not have some Marines out there handling it?"

Benny was slowly scratching his chin as he contemplated Jack's words while looking back at Mac.

"He's right Mac, that location is all wrong for some kind of diplomatic compound. Hell, it feels more like…like Spook work."

Mac's eyebrows rose slightly at the possibility of the property they appeared to be placed here to do surveillance on could be some kind of CIA operation. Of the many assignments he and his crew had been given over the years, one involving spying on the spies would be a first.

"I'm calling Tilley."

Mac walked back into the bedroom as he placed the call. This time, Tilley picked up on the first ring.

"You inside?"

Tilley was getting right to it.

"Yeah – we're upstairs looking out at our neighbors."

Tilley paused briefly.

"Good. You already know what you're there for then."

Mac stood in the middle of the bedroom with the cell phone to his ear while slowly shaking his head at Tilley's words.

"No, not really. What should we tell you about the neighbors?"

Again Tilley paused briefly before answering.

"Keep your eyes on them 24/7. Keep mental notes on who is coming and going, how long they stay, when they leave, basic surveillance operation Mac. Easy money."

Something about how Tilley said that last part made Mac uneasy. His instincts were what had kept him alive all these years, and they were once again warning him something wasn't quite right.

"One of our rigs just went in while I was watching, not more than ten minutes ago."

"What?"

Mac had surprised Tilley with that information.

"I said one of ours...from State, just arrived at the location."

Tilley recovered quickly from being caught off guard, this time not hesitating to reply.

"Ok, good...that's the kind of information I want from you and your team Mac. Who goes in, how long they stay. Do it in shifts, but make sure you always have at least one set of eyes on them at all times. Now downstairs, in the kitchen, there's a door to the pantry. Go inside there and you should be able to find an access panel. Follow the stairs down and check it out, but not all of you at once. Remember, keep at least one set of eyes on your neighbor at all times Mac. Always."

"When do you tell me the rest of it Tilley? Tell me why we're really sitting out here?"

"I have to keep you on need to know for a while Mac. Sorry, but I'm not even sure of all the what's and why's on this one. Just go check out the pantry access, and then stay put. That's it. That's all I have for you right now."

That was the second time during the same conversation Tilley said something that sent the warning bells in Mac's head ringing loud and clear. Since when did Tilley not know every detail of an assignment? Before Mac could raise his objections, Tilley ended the call.

Jack stepped into the bedroom and tipped his head in the direction of the balcony.

"So is that what the four of us are doing here? Watching the compound across the road?"

Mac nodded as Jack's mouth curled downward in disgust.

"This ain't right Mac. You know it too. Right from the get go, this ain't been right. No way the four of us get sent all the way out here to do simple surveillance. I mean, what the hell? Why pay us this kind of money for that? There's tons of people who could do this for a lot less. No way…we're here for something else. Tilley give any clues?"

Mac shook his head.

"No – nothing. Said he just wants surveillance, 24/7."

Mac walked back out to the balcony and told Minnick to continue watching the compound. He then had Benny and Jack follow him downstairs to the kitchen where he located the pantry door.

"Tilley said there's an access panel inside here that leads to a stairwell."

Minnick was the first to spot the panel, partially hidden behind a large stand up freezer.

"There – behind the freezer. You can see the cut-out in the wall."

Jack pushed the freezer to the side, exposing the five by five cut-out Minnick had indicated. Mac placed both hands against the panel and pushed inward. The panel opened easily, and just as Tilley had described, revealed a narrow set of stairs that led down. A series of LED lights that hung along the walls of the stairs illuminated the way. The three men made their way downward, the stairs opening into a small, low ceilinged cellar area with a dirt floor, and rough textured concrete walls. It reminded Mac of a bomb shelter. In the middle of the room sat a single, large wooden table.

"Holy shit."

Benny's reaction represented Mac and Jack's feelings as well regarding the contents neatly organized atop the table.

XII.

Ray Tilley was not used to being so unsettled, but that is exactly what the last few phone conversations with Mac Walker did to him. Mac and his team were sent out to conduct surveillance on a potential post-Gaddafi gunrunning operation, with the possibility of an eventual subject termination order. Why the hell then did Mardian have them set up across the road from a location that appeared to be run by our own State Department? And who was this Mark Densmore Mac mentioned, who he said is, or was, with the FBI? Tilley had reached out to a State Department contact to try and get someone over to Ella's office to assist Mac and his team. Was Densmore the one who they sent out?

As for whatever happened with Moretti, why he would have sold out Mac's team to whoever was gunning for them, Tilley was in the dark on that as well. As always when working with foreign agents who he didn't know well, Tilley had taken precautions. The safe house Moretti was delivering Mac and his team to was a temporary location. The primary safe house for the assignment had been unknown to Moretti, meaning Mac and his team, now that they had arrived at that safe house, should be able to proceed with the mission as planned. Unless of course, someone else they trusted was working against them as well. That left few remaining options though. There was Mardian and his Congressional contacts. There was Tilley's source at the State Department who he had already reached out to. And Ella Lerner and her security team. Of those, it was Mardian who Tilley trusted least, and Mardian did know of Moretti.

It wasn't fair to Mac and his men that he couldn't give them answers. It wasn't fair, but more important – it was dangerous. Ray Tilley knew his line of work involved dealing with shits. Washington D.C. was crawling with them, but that didn't mean he left an entire team hanging in the middle of a place like Benghazi without clueing them in on what was really going on. That wasn't right, and Tilley had no intention of letting that scenario sit.

He was going to have to go see Mardian.

Tilley picked up his phone and dialed Mardian's secure contact number – the one Mardian always picked up. Always.

This time, there was no answer.

Tilley sat as his desk pondering his next move. Mac and his men were in no immediate danger, they had their surveillance instructions, and once they made their way to the cellar, they would realize there was more to the assignment than just surveillance. Mac would be calling him back demanding answers – answers that Tilley felt compelled to provide him. Answers though, that he simply did not have at this moment.

Another call was placed to Mardian. Again, Mardian failed to pick up.

Tilley decided to reach out to his mentor, retired Army General Martin Vannatter. General Vannatter had earned the rank of four stars shortly before his retirement from the military at age sixty five. That was just over ten years ago. Though no longer in the day to day game of high ranking military politics, the general had maintained an impressive array of contacts, and he and Tilley continued regular communications with each other. Tilley had spent several years as part of the general's staff, a job which had given Tilley direct access to some of the most powerful figures in Washington D.C. and led to his current working relationship with Stephen Mardian.

The general picked up on the second ring.

"Hello Mr. Tilley. It's a bit late, so I assume you're in a bit of a pickle. How can I help?"

General Vannatter had long been known for his ability to somehow know what a situation was, and what is wasn't. He read people almost instantly, and that initial reading was almost always proven right. More important, General Vannatter could be trusted. He kept a myriad of secrets, never indicated a desire to cash out and write a book, and gave every indication of taking those secrets to the grave.

"That will allow me to remain alive well into my dementia years Mr. Tilley."

That was the comment the general repeated to Tilley often during the months before his retirement. Tilley was hoping the general could now give him some insight, or even some actual real time information, about what might really be going on in Benghazi.

"Thank you for taking my call general. I have a team just arrived in Benghazi."

Tilley paused, knowing the general would have something to say about that. He was slightly surprised at what little he did have to say.

'Ok. Go ahead..."

Tilley's mind scrambled to present the situation with as much, and as little, detail as possible. That was how the general demanded things. He didn't like unnecessary information. Just the essential facts, or shut the hell up and move along.

"It's a four man team. I was told it was primarily surveillance with the possibility of a termination order. Illegal weapons related - nothing out of the ordinary there. Thing is general, it seems the location being watched is uh... possibly linked with our own State Department. And, one of the team is convinced they saw an individual who was, or is, FBI."

The general said nothing, but Tilley could picture the older man sitting in his spacious home office at his farm estate a few miles outside of Spencer, West Virginia, the place of his birth nearly seventy six years ago, looking up at the ceiling as he processed the information Tilley had just told him.

"This team of yours – they are good? Would you say, among the best you have?"

"Yes – absolutely."

Again the general paused for a moment.

"So what is it about this team Mr. Tilley that makes them the best? Beyond the ability to fire a weapon and the like, what is it that allows you to place your trust in them to complete the assignment?"

Now it was Tilley's turn to pause as he thought over what it was about Mac Walker and his men that made them his first choice when an assignment became available.

"They get it done. No muss and no fuss."

Tilley could almost hear over the phone the general's mouth spreading into a smile.

"Would you say they do so without question? That they don't suffer from certain...moral indecisiveness when it comes to, as you put it, getting it done?"

Tilley found himself nodding as he sat alone in his own office.

"Yes. They don't question. At least not yet. We give them the assignment, and they do it."

"There's your answer Mr. Tilley – at least part of it."

Tilley knew he was missing something that was right in front of him. Something the general expected him to now realize without having to be told.

"I'm sorry general, I'm not following."

"Mr. Tilley, it was no accident you were chosen to present this particular assignment to that particular team of men – this team that you describe as being capable of simply getting the assignment done without question. No muss and no fuss, right?"

Tilley remained confused.

"That's correct."

"Ok then Mr. Tilley, that would indicate that this assignment will likely present a certain moral conflict. A moral conflict that would be problematic to a team less inclined to simply get it done, as you put it. A moral conflict that it would appear, based on what you have just told me, involve operatives within out own government."

A creeping understanding presented itself to Ray Tilley – and it left him cold.

"I sense you are now beginning to understand Mr. Tilley."

Tilley rested his head against the palm of his right hand as he took a slow, measured breath.

"I do."

"Very well Mr. Tilley. Feel free to call me anytime. I will be curious to hear of the outcome on this."

Ray Tilley cleared his throat, feeling the stress of the realization begin to build within him.

"Thank you general. I'll do that. Please take care sir."

General Vannatter's tone changed slightly as he responded, clearly indicating to Tilley he was now swimming in some very deep, dark, and dangerous waters.

"You be very careful Mr. Tilley. Very-very careful."

Tilley put his cell phone down on his desk, feeling his shoulders slump forward and the unmistakable pulsing of a headache soon to arrive. The general was likely right – as he almost always was. A serious moral conflict was about to present itself.

Mac Walker and his men were not sent to Benghazi on a simple surveillance assignment. Mac Walker was sent there to kill Americans.

XIII.

Mac looked down at the table where four identical AS-50 sniper rifles were neatly lined up with corresponding and quite deadly fifty caliber armor piercing incendiary explosive rounds of ammunition. There was enough boxed ammo on the table to engage in a firefight for several hours.

Benny picked up one of the rifles and looked it over carefully.

"These are the real things Mac. Beautiful! Makes me feel a whole lot safer knowing we are working with this kind of firepower. From close range I could blow a hole in a damn tank with one of these. Each one has a night vision scope too. This is some serious business, man."

Jack was looking at Mac as the both of them realized what these particular weapons meant regarding the kind of assignment they were really engaged in.

"Mac, we aren't here for surveillance, are we?"

Mac picked up one of the sniper rifles, raised it to his face, and looked through the Yukon scope. Mac didn't recognize the model, which meant it was very new, and likely very good.

"No Jack, looks like we might be doing a lot more than just keeping an eye on the neighbors."

Jack's agitation returned, stronger than ever.

"For fuck's sake Mac – those are Americans driving into that compound over there! What the hell…they want us to kill off some of our own? We don't do that Mac – we're the good guys!"

Mac offered a thin smile, though the effort almost hurt his face to do it.

"Are we the good guys Jack? It's getting harder to tell these days. Look, no sense thinking something that hasn't been confirmed yet. I just spoke with Tilley and all he said was to keep an eye on the activity across the road and report back to him. That's it. Maybe these guns are just…precautionary measures."

Jack stepped toward Mac, his eyes flaring open as he pointed back down to the table of weapons.

"C'mon Mac! Don't bullshit me! Those sniper rifles mean one fucking thing – we are supposed to take someone down, and so far, the only place we have access to, is that diplomatic compound, or whatever the hell it is, a few hundred yards from our location. We don't have transportation Mac! They stuck us here with no way out just waiting for them to green light the termination order. You know it, I know it, anyone with half a fucking mind knows it! And then what Mac? Let's say we kill who they want us to kill. How the hell do we get out of here? Fucking hitchhike? What the hell is going on? This is all too sloppy, which means it's too dangerous. You need to shut this thing down Mac. Like right fucking now."

Mac could feel his own anger rising up in him as he stared back at Jack while Benny's smiling presence attempted to step between the two men.

"Don't take that tone with me Jack. You know better. Don't piss me off."

Jack attempted to take another step toward Mac, but Benny placed both of his hands against the larger man's chest and gently pushed him back.

"No-no-no, we don't go chewing our own legs off boys. Now everyone needs to calm down, ok?"

Jack's right hand moved downward with enough force to push Benny's own hands away from him.

"Get the fuck out of my way Benny."

Benny's smile remained, though his eyes indicated otherwise.

"Or what Jack? You want to try me? Really?"

Benny Williamson, though a chronically cheerful man in even the most stressful of circumstances, was no-one to push into a physical confrontation. Jack knew that, and respected it. He had seen the results of those who didn't respect it – and it was never pretty. That said, Jack remained furious at how Mac had given them an assignment that left them all with far more questions than answers.

"You got to be just as worried as I am Benny. This ain't your first rodeo – you know this thing is going down all wrong, starting with us doing work for the fucking United Nations."

Benny's reply was slow and relaxed, his tone working to calm Jack's nerves, though his words were also intended to let Mac know he agreed with much of what Jack was worried about.

"I hear you Jack, and I get what you're saying, man. At this point though, our options are pretty limited, and we ain't been told to kill nobody just yet. So for now, everyone needs to keep their shit together, and work together, am I right?"

Jack's eyes stared back at Mac before settling on Benny's still smiling face.

"Yeah, you're right."

Benny stepped back from Jack and then turned to face Mac.

"So what's the call Mac? You really just gonna have us sitting around here spying on that house? Is that really all Tilley wants us to do?"

Mac shrugged.

"Yeah – for now. I asked him for more information, but he said that we were on a need to know status."

The smile left Benny's face.

"Need to know? Since when does Tilley say something like that to us?"

Jack spoke from behind Benny.

"Since never. I'll say it again, it all points to this whole thing not feeling right."

Benny shook a finger at Mac, the smile returning.

"What it means is our own Ray Tilley is almost as much in the dark about this assignment as we are. He's still trying to do right by us Mac, I don't doubt that."

Mac said nothing in response, knowing he didn't feel the same, his trust of Tilley already greatly diminished. As much as Jack was pissed at him, Mac was feeling nearly as upset over this assignment as the big guy from Alabama was.

Shit wasn't right.

XIV.

Ray Tilley navigated his silver BMW 750iL in and around the typically congested D.C. traffic on his way to Mardian's office at 19th and G. If Mardian refused to reply to his phone calls, then Tilley had no choice but to take his questions to him in person.

It was nearly the noon hour by the time Tilley pulled his car alongside one of the parking spaces in front of Mardian's three story red bricked building. Two men and a woman were walking out the front door. Mardian's personal office was the entire top floor of the building. Tilley had only been up there a handful of times over the years.

Walking into the reception area, Tilley smiled casually at the attractive, dark haired woman who sat behind the large, cherry wood reception desk. She smiled back, asking if he had an appointment.

"I'm here to see Mr. Mardian – upstairs. I know the way."

The woman's smile disappeared, and when the two armed men emerged from somewhere behind him, Tilley guessed the receptionist had activated a silent alarm.

The shorter of the two security personnel asked Tilley if he had an appointment to see Mr. Mardian.

"Don't need one. Mardian knows who I am."

Tilley peered up toward the ceiling, scanning for where the security cameras were located. He spotted one in a far corner adjacent to the elevator entrance.

"Let's go Mardian – I'm not leaving until I see you. I'm coming up."

As Tilley moved toward the elevator, the taller of Mardian's two man security team grabbed the back of his arm and pulled him back.

"That isn't allowed sir – please take a seat over here."

Tilley shook his arm from the man's grip and stepped toward the ten foot long dark leather couch that ran the length of the reception room wall opposite the reception desk.

"You tell Mardian we need to talk. Now."

Mardian's receptionist was on the phone, likely already speaking with him. Her eyes glanced at Tilley several times as she whispered into the receiver, her head nodding.

"Mr. Tilley, Mr. Mardian says you are welcome to join him in his office upstairs."

Tilley swept past the two security personnel before pausing as he sensed both of them intended to follow him into the elevator.

"I know the fucking way. You two can stay down here."

One of the men put his hand up to his ear, listening as Mardian instructed him to allow Tilley to come up alone. Both of Mardian's security detail stood motionless, staring at Tilley as he turned back around and entered the elevator, his hand slamming the third floor button.

The elevator opened up to a small six by six room with a single, steel framed door opposite the elevator. A red button was housed to the left of the door which Tilley quickly pushed. There was a faint buzzing followed by the door's interior mechanism unlocking as the door opened a few inches inward. Tilley pushed it further open and stepped into the office of Stephen Mardian.

"Not one fucking word Tilley. Sit your ass down and shut up."

Tilley looked across the large room where Mardian sat behind a huge, black metallic framed desk. Two matching chairs sat just in front of the desk, one of which Mardian demanded Tilley now sit down in.

"Why didn't you answer my calls Mardian? Why didn't you call me back?"

Mardian stood up, his expensive, custom tailored dark grey suit not enough to mask his short and rounded body.

"I told you not a fucking word until you sit down. So-sit-the-fuck-down."

Stephen Mardian was well known for his abrasive personality, the kind of abrasiveness that was the result of being born into old D.C. money and power without having to earn it. Politically, he was, and had been for some time, a very formidable figure. His balding head and fleshy face that always appeared on the verge of breaking out into a substantial sweat, lent the D.C. power broker a somewhat comical appearance, which likely caused further frustration-induced abrasiveness. Mardian demanded people respect him.

Sitting down across from him, Tilley noted Mardian was on edge. Something was troubling him – something significant.

"I didn't call you back for a couple reasons Tilley. One, I don't have the answers. Two, I don't know if I can trust you. This Moretti thing, I don't know what went down with that. Why he turned on your team.

You took precautions though, right? With the safe house, like you normally do?"

Tilley nodded.

"Yeah – the assignment is still operational."

Mardian ran his short fingered hands across his brow and then down the front of his face.

"Good. Until I know more, we just keep this thing going as instructed. So tell me Tilley, how'd you get the team to the safe house? Who took care of that for you?"

Tilley looked coolly back at Mardian, hoping his face betrayed no information.

"Had a contact there. Called in a favor."

Mardian leaned forward, his elbows sitting atop his desk.

"Who was it? I need to know who you involved in this."

Tilley took a deep breath as he rolled his head from side to side trying to work a stress kink from his neck.

"How about you tell me where you're getting your instructions from. Is it the woman from the United Nations? Dasha? Is she the one who's got you so rattled Mardian?"

Mardian's eyes flashed anger, feeling Tilley was disrespecting him.

"I'm not rattled. And I don't need to tell you who I'm answering to on this one, but you do need to answer to me Tilley. Don't forget that."

Tilley folded his arms across his chest, again sensing how nervous Mardian actually was.

"Right now I'm most concerned with keeping my team safe. They want answers, and so do I. If you can't give them to me, then I'm gonna pull the plug. Terminate the assignment and bring them home."

Mardian's forehead was now covered in a thin layer of sweat despite the building's air conditioning keeping the interior temperature well below seventy degrees.

"No you won't Tilley. That's not an option. You try and do that and it'll be a death warrant for that team, every one of them. They'll never make it back."

Tilley felt his rage welling up inside of him. Was Mardian actually threatening Mac and his men?

"You threatening my team Mardian?"

Stephen Mardian's eyes looked down as he slowly shook his head.

"No...the threat isn't from me Tilley. It is real though. If your team doesn't take care of business over there, they won't be allowed to come back. We're dealing with some very powerful people on this one."

Tilley's mind swirled with questions. He had always considered Mardian a very powerful person. Who or what could have him so spooked?

"What is that compound you have my team watching? Is it some kind of diplomatic site? A location just outside the city to allow off the record meetings between U.S. officials and local tribal groups?"

Mardian's eyes remained lowered, sweat now beginning to pool just above his brows.

"Something like that. As far as I know, but also what you've already been told. There's an allegation of some gunrunning going on, you know, people trying to make a quick buck. That's how it was presented to me at first. Keep an eye on them, try to confirm weapons transfers. No big deal really."

Tilley shook his head.

"Bullshit Mardian. C'mon, you don't send someone like Mac Walker and his team to look through a pair of fucking binoculars. And what about the sniper rifles we left them? Those just for surveillance too? Hell no. This thing reeks of a kill order. The question is, who are we supposed to kill – and why?"

Mardian raised his eyes to look back at Tilley.

"I don't have those answers."

Tilley's voice rose in anger.

"Stop fucking lying to me Mardian! That's what's got you so scared right now. You know who the kill order is for, don't you? You just found out. They sent us over there without that information, so that my team would have no fucking choice but to carry out the assignment, or they don't get back home. That means it's a big deal. Whoever we are supposed to take out, it's not some Muslim radical. It's not some corrupt Libyan official. This person is one of ours. They're American, and they must be connected. So you tell me who it is, and why."

The corner of Mardian's mouth was trembling slightly as a droplet of sweat fell from his brow and onto his desk.

"I don't know. It's not confirmed. And there is no kill order Tilley. Not yet. Your team is doing surveillance – that's it."

"Why Mac Walker? Why his team? Can you at least tell me that, Mardian?"

Stephen Mardian wiped his brow with his right hand as he sat up in his chair.

"Because they get things done. That's it. No big mystery. They take an assignment and they go out and do it. No questions."

Mardian's description of why Mac was chosen for the assignment was the same description given to him by the general – because Mac and his team handled things efficiently and without question, without concern over moral conflicts. That meant such a conflict, as Tilley had already suspected, was most certainly on its way.

"So that's it – you're not going to tell me more?"

Mardian shook his head, his usual contempt for anyone who questioned him returning.

"I'll let you know what you need to know Tilley. No more. That's how it's always worked. As soon as I have something I need to tell you, I will. In the meantime, don't call me, and sure as hell don't show up here. Got it?"

Tilley stood up and began walking out of Mardian's office. He gave his answer without looking back.

"Fuck you Mardian."

During the drive back home Tilley's phone rang. It was the general.

"Hello Mr. Tilley. I went ahead and made a few calls on what may or may not be going on in Benghazi these days. You have a minute?"

Tilley pulled the car over to the side of the road.

"Yes sir – go ahead."

"Well...there is a ton of CIA activity down there. Now what's interesting to me is that there's little of that kind of activity in Tripoli, which normally you would think that's where all the acronyms would be running around. Not so. Benghazi has CIA, NSA, British intelligence, Italian intelligence, the Russians and Chinese have people on the ground there, Turkey, the Saudis, and perhaps most interesting, a significant uptick in U.N. SitCen activity around there."

Tilley wasn't sure what the general was referring to when he mentioned SitCen.

"Sir, what is the U.N.'s SitCen?"

The general cleared his throat. Tilley could tell the retired military man was enjoying this cloak and dagger stuff.

"Their Situation Center. It was developed in the 1990's. It coordinates with all of the intelligence agencies in the world, at least all the major ones. They have what are called Information and Research officers who work within the SitCen. These people have access to…well to everywhere. And right now, they are crawling all over Benghazi apparently. Not Tripoli – Benghazi."

"Why?"

General Vannatter paused for a moment before answering.

"Don't know that Mr. Tilley. Wish I did, because it sure does seem peculiar. Now something I forgot to mention regarding SitCen and what they do. What they are probably doing in Benghazi. One of their primary directives, especially in more recent years, is monitoring arms trafficking throughout the world."

Tilley was nodding his head as he sat in his car, the sound of passing vehicles threatening to drown out the general's words.

"Ok – yeah. That makes sense, because that's what my team is doing in Benghazi. At least that's what I've been told. They're monitoring potential arms dealing. Am I missing the significance here?"

The general continued.

"The significance is that, according to my source, the whole department is rampant with people connected to arms dealing. That they aren't just monitoring weapons distribution, they're trying to control it. They're organizing it."

The concept shocked Tilley – and he didn't shock easily.

"What? The U.N. is dealing in weapons? Why?"

The general's tone softened just a bit, as if he was growing tired.

"Well, the way it was put to me was that it was a newer program for...I'm trying to remember how he said it. It was a new program for a New United Nations. Something like that."

Tilley felt a headache coming on fast. He remembered Dasha Al Marri, when explaining the assignment to Mac, using the exact description of the need for a New United Nations.

"General, could you do me another favor? I'm sorry for the bother sir but...I could use the help."

The general's response was immediate and no longer sounded tired.

"Absolutely Mr. Tilley. Whatever you need."

"It's a name. Can you have someone run a check on her? The name is Dasha Al Marri."

Tilley could hear General Vannatter's breathing quicken.

"Dasha Al Marri? I knew her father. High ranking official in the Dubai government. Oil money – and lots of it. He was a big part of the relationship between Venezuela and the United Arab Emirates. Rumor was that a good chunk of all those Venezuelan oil profits went right back to the Arabs."

Tilley pressed for more information.

"Anything else you know about her?"

"No, like I said, knew her father. I can have her checked out though. She involved in this Benghazi assignment of yours?"

Tilley glanced in his rearview mirror, believing he saw a car pulling behind him. Nothing was there though.

"Yeah, she's basically putting up the funds. At least, that's how I understand it. She's with the U.N."

The general chuckled.

"Way we seem to be heading, every man woman and child is going to be answering to the U.N. whether they want to or not."

Tilley glanced back in his rearview mirror again.

Someone was behind his car.

XV.

"So what's the plan Mac?"

Mac looked at Benny again, appreciative of how he was working to diffuse the growing animosity with Jack.

"Like you said Benny – we keep our shit together. We watch the compound across the street and report back to Tilley. That's the assignment. If we get termination orders, then…well, we'll deal with that when we need to. For now, we'll just be fucking house sitters."

Benny looked over at Jack, who continued to glare back at Mac.

"That sound ok with you Alabama?"

Jack raised himself up to his full height of six foot three and inhaled deeply while closing his eyes. When his eyes re-opened he shrugged and offered a small smile.

"Yeah – whatever. Like you said, we haven't been told to kill anyone yet, so at this point, we're just doing surveillance. If they want to pay us for that, then that's fine by me. I don't believe for a second that's what this is about, but for now, that's what this is about, so fuck it."

Mac heard a shrill whistle coming from upstairs. It was Minnick signaling them.

Jack grabbed one of the sniper rifles and bounded upstairs, taking the steps three at a time as Mac and Benny followed close behind. They arrived in the upstairs bedroom where Minnick remained watching the compound from the balcony through one of the pairs of military grade high powered binoculars as he described what he was seeing.

"More vehicles entering the compound. Three large transport trucks, all with United Nations Food Relief identifications on them. There's an unmarked black sedan in the front and another one in the back. Drivers of the transport trucks appear to be Middle Eastern, possibly Libyan, the drivers of the sedans are white. All the vehicles are now parked in front of the compound entrance. There's at least nine or ten individuals moving around the facility. They appear to be unloading crates. Can't quite make out the identification on the crates, but I think they're the same United Nations Food Relief emblems that are on the transport trucks."

Mac stepped next to Minnick who then handed him another pair of binoculars. Looking through them, he was able to confirm what Minnick had just reported. Mac paid particular attention to the three white men who he assumed had emerged from the unmarked black sedans.

"Those guys are definitely some of ours. Possibly CIA. Were there three or four who came out of the sedans?"

Minnick lowered his binoculars and rubbed his eyes.

"Four. The other one went inside the main house of the compound."

Mac focused the binoculars on the main house entrance, waiting to see who would walk out. He was rewarded moments later with the figure of Mark Densmore bounding down the stone entrance steps – the same man they had seen outside Ella's building in Benghazi. A man Mac last knew to be an FBI agent.

Walking alongside Densmore was a well dressed white man who appeared to be in his late forties. He was of slight build, but moved gracefully, and with purpose. It was the movement one acquires from certain training. Movement Mac most often associated with CIA. Minnick was thinking the same thing.

"The guy on the left reeks of CIA Mac."

Mac lowered his binoculars and stepped back into the bedroom.

"Yeah, he sure does. The other one he's walking next to is a guy named Mark Densmore. Last I knew of him, he was FBI. He was at the little riot of ours in Benghazi. One of them who pulled up in the SUVs."

Benny stepped onto the balcony, grabbing Mac's binoculars as he did so.

"And you say he's FBI? Did you tell Tilley about him?"

Mac nodded as his mind worked out the possible scenarios of what was going on in that compound across the road. The food relief trucks were clearly a ruse. The chances of them carrying weapons would seem likely. The CIA's involvement was not so surprising either. Shifting weapons around the globe was not uncommon for that organization as they worked to topple one regime and build up another. It was Densmore's presence in Benghazi that Mac found most odd.

"Yeah, I told Tilley. He said he'd get back to me on it."

Minnick's hand motioned to Mac.

"Gonna want to see this. Mr. CIA and the other guy are having words."

Mac moved quickly back to the balcony as Minnick handed him his binoculars. Just as described, Mark Densmore and the other man who they believed to be CIA were nearly nose to nose at the bottom of the main house steps. Mac noted how it was Densmore who appeared to be the more dominant presence, and he was soon proven correct as the other man stepped back and lowered his head, clearly communicating a more passive position.

"Looks like Densmore's in charge over there."

Benny, who was also watching the brief altercation between the two men, concurred.

"No doubt about that."

The sedans and transport trucks were already making their way back out of the compound, pulling out onto the road at considerable speed. Mac focused his binoculars on Densmore, who sat in the passenger seat of the trailing black sedan. As Mac did so, Densmore's head turned and he appeared to be looking directly back at Mac through the vehicle's passenger window. The distance between them was nearly three hundred yards apart, so Mac knew the other man couldn't actually see him, but Densmore continued to stare at Mac's location on the safe house balcony.

Benny lowered his binoculars and glanced at Mac.

"You see that? He was looking right at us. He knows we're here."

Mac knew Benny was right. Though he may not have been able to see them clearly, Mark Densmore just sent them a message. He knew the compound was being watched and he just let them know he knew.

Now if only I could figure out what the hell that means.

"I'd love to be able to follow those vehicles and see where they're going."

Mac's mind struggled momentarily to refocus on Benny's words.

"What?"

Benny tipped his head in the direction of the departing transport trucks and black sedans.

"It would be nice to know where they are coming from. My guess would be the airport since they had those U.N. markings, but then again, who knows?"

Benny's reference to the Benghazi airport snapped a name back into Mac's head.

Louis Danton – the name Angelo Moretti had given me in case something went wrong with the assignment and we needed to get out of Benghazi fast. Moretti had described Danton as the ranking U.N. humanitarian official at the Benina Airport.

Given Danton's name came from Moretti, who had tried to have Mac's team killed after they left the airport, meant he couldn't be trusted of course, but knowing more about who he was and what his true purpose in Benghazi could be would go a long way toward giving Mac and his team some much needed answers and improve their chances of getting out of this assignment alive.

Mac decided that at that point, he and his team needed two things. First, was a mode of transportation, and second, was a person who they could trust for information who had on the ground experience here in Benghazi. Mac could think of only one person to possibly meet that need – Ella Lerner.

Mac walked back into the bedroom and folded his arms across his chest.

"Listen up gentlemen. We have some work to do tonight. We need a vehicle, and then we need to reach out to Ella again. I'm pretty sure she has some answers for us."

Jack grinned. It was nice to see the big man eager to do something.

"A little recon Mac?"

Mac nodded.

"Something like that. You wanna help me to secure the vehicle Jack?"

Jack's grin grew wider.

"Hell yeah – better than sitting around here. What do you have in mind?"

Mac's eyes wandered back toward the balcony outside.

"This neighborhood has a lot of upscale homes. Some of them are sure to be vacant, with cars parked inside garages. We find one those, and bring the car back here. Simple plan for simple minds, right?'

Jack's eyes openly communicated his approval.

"Simple-simple-simple is how I like it Mac."

Mac looked to Benny and Minnick.

"You two will stay back here. I want one set of eyes on the compound, and the other guy providing security for our position. We have night vision capability, so no excuses - no surprises. Densmore made it clear he knows we're here, and what exactly that means isn't clear, so until then, we are seriously watching each other's backs."

Mac glanced down at his watch.

"A few more hours till nightfall, then you and me are on the move Jack."

XVI.

Tilley watched the form of a man slowly moving toward the driver's side of his BMW. Whoever it was, he didn't appear too concerned about concealing his approach, so Tilley assumed the man posed no real immediate threat to him. Glancing out his right rearview mirror, Tilley was able to spot the man's vehicle parked behind his own, but farther off to the right side of the road. It was a newer, black Mercedes sedan.

A hand rapped lightly on the BMW's driver side window. Tilley lowered the window halfway, his eyes looking up at an unsmiling and very familiar face. It was Nigel, head of security for Dasha Al Marri, the woman responsible for funding Mac Walker's assignment in Benghazi.

"Hello Mr. Tilley. Dasha would very much like you to join her for a brief conversation in her car. Please do not bring any weapons with you."

Tilley tried hard to appear casual, but he could feel his heart pounding in his chest as he responded to Nigel's request.

"I'm not armed, but I am a bit busy. Will this take long?"

Nigel's face remained unreadable, his eyes looking back down at Tilley without emotion.

"It will take however long Dasha wishes it to take Mr. Tilley. Please…let me escort you to the car."

Something in the tone of Nigel's voice convinced Tilley he had no choice but to comply. Turning the BMW's engine off, Tilley opened the door and stepped outside as D.C. traffic continued to drive past.

"Right this way Mr. Tilley."

Nigel, though shorter than Tilley, gave off the aura of a man quite capable and more than willing, to kill. Tilley knew the type well – he considered Mac and his team to be cut from a very similar cloth. Nigel opened the left rear passenger door and motioned for Tilley to step inside.

Dasha sat resplendent in a silver designer jacket and matching pants, her dark hair again tied neatly behind her head in a tight bun. As

Tilley looked at her and attempted a smile, Dasha's eyes indicated she was in no mood for a friendly chat.

"This morning I was in my apartment in New York Mr. Tilley, very much enjoying NOT being in this pig shit hole of a city. Do you know why I am here now, sitting with you having this ridiculous conversation Mr. Tilley?"

Ray Tilley shook his head.

"No Ms...uh...Dasha. No I don't. I assume it's related to the Benghazi assignment."

Dasha's lips curled into a sneer as she leaned toward Tilley, her dark eyes smoldering with just-under-the-surface rage.

"Yes Mr. Tilley – it most certainly is related to the Benghazi assignment, as you call it. I was told to return here to speak with you personally, so that I can communicate to you in no uncertain terms, how very much my organization is expecting your team to complete their assignment per our agreement. I don't appreciate having to be bothered with such things Mr. Tilley. Not one bit."

Ray Tilley found his own anger now emerging.

Who the hell does this woman think she is?

"Maybe you could let me know exactly what it is we are supposed to be doing in Benghazi so my team has a better chance of meeting that obligation. It seems clear now that it intends to go beyond a simple surveillance operation."

Dasha leaned back into her seat, her perfectly manicured hands folding gracefully over her crossed legs.

"Yes Mr. Tilley, it quite possibly will involve more than surveillance. You knew that to be a possibility from the beginning. Why then are you now bothering Mr. Mardian with questions and threats of bringing your team home prior to completion of the assignment?"

Tilley didn't back down, now turning himself toward Dasha, his voice, though not shouting, increasing in volume.

"Because if you expect us to kill Americans Dasha, you better damn well let us know who and more importantly, why. So far, you haven't told us shit, and I've got four men sitting in that hellhole of Benghazi wondering what the hell is going on! I want answers – and they deserve answers!"

Dasha managed to make her responding smile to Tilley appear almost warm, though her eyes remained near furious.

"It is as I told you before Mr. Tilley. We are to be monitoring a possible arms dealing operation. A very significant operation I might add, one that my group at the New United Nations has taken a particular interest in."

Tilley cocked his head to the side, his eyes squinting slightly.

"You mean the United Nations, right? You said New United Nations."

Dasha smiled, and this time even her eyes appeared to fill with warmth.

"Yes, I did. The assignment is simple Mr. Tilley - monitor the activity at the compound which your men are to now be residing across the road from. They report to you, and you in turn report that information directly back to Mr. Mardian. I am having a terrible time comprehending what is so difficult to understand about such an assignment."

"Because it's bullshit. That's not the assignment. We left Mac and his men weapons that are tools for assassinations. It's a kill order you plan to give us, and I think you always planned to do so. Problem is, everything is pointing to my team being ordered to kill other Americans, and I need to know why before I relay that kind of order. I'm having a terrible time comprehending what is so difficult to understand about THAT."

Dasha looked out her own passenger window, her voice coming back toward Tilley like very dark, deep, and slow moving water.

"If you value the lives of your men Mr. Tilley, you will do as I ask. They are to complete the assignment as ordered, and if those orders evolve into more, shall we say, direct action against others in Benghazi, then so be it. That is why they are there. Failure to do so at any time will result in their own termination, as well as others involved. Do you understand what I'm saying to Mr. Tilley?"

Ray Tilley looked over at Dasha Al Marri and actually contemplated if he could manage to choke her to death before Virgil came to her aid. It was a foolish thought, and he quickly pushed it out of his mind.

"I understand the threat Dasha. Mardian already gave me a similar one."

Dasha placed her left hand on top of Tilley's right knee and lightly squeezed it.

"Good then Mr. Tilley. We understand each other perfectly now."

Tilley paused, his mind uncertain if he should finish the conversation with a question that now floated around his mind.

"I'm wondering something Dasha. After the night you spent with Mac, would you really kill him and his men off that easy? That time together doesn't mean anything to you?"

Dasha put a hand to her mouth, trying to stifle her laughter.

"Oh my Mr. Tilley, it appears you are some kind of silly, hopeless romantic! I actually don't particularly care for men – but am more than happy to fuck them, your Mr. Walker included."

XVII.

Mac and Jack had been walking in the dark for nearly three miles, each of them carrying one of the fifty caliber sniper rifles on their backs. What little traffic that came down the dirt and gravel road was avoided by the two men jumping down into the shallow drainage ditches that ran along each side of the road and pressing their bodies flat against the ground. Mac, knowing Jack had a fear of snakes, couldn't help but take the opportunity to have a little fun.

"Hey Alabama, if you land on top of one those dessert vipers they say are crawling all over this place, just remain calm, ok?"

Jack jumped so quickly out of the ditch he appeared to be momentarily flying.

"Goddammit Mac, why'd you have to go and say that?"

Mac was trying very hard not to laugh, while he moved back onto the road and stood next to Jack.

"Hey, just letting you know there are a few creepy crawlies out here. It's nighttime though, they're probably all slow and sleepy by now. No worries big guy. Except the scorpions, those little bastards love hunting at night."

Jack glared back at Mac, shaking his head.

"Asshole."

Mac was about to respond when the glow of headlights began to illuminate the road again, forcing him and Jack back down into the ditch, something Jack was far less eager to do after Mac's earlier warning of snakes.

The first vehicle was another United Nations food relief transport truck. Three more identical trucks followed, driving slowly down the road back toward the compound Mac and his men had been ordered to conduct surveillance on.

"You see those drivers Mac? They sure looked Libyan to me. The serious business kind. Those weren't some save the world United Nations types."

Mac nodded at Jack's description while his eyes followed the path of the departing trucks, their taillights glowing like an increasingly distant, red eyed demon.

"Look at that – they're turning off the main road. That's well before our position across the road from the compound. Now where do you suppose they're going now?"

Both Mac and Jack raised their night vision binoculars to follow the path of the U.N. food relief trucks as they continued down a secondary road before finally disappearing from view.

"Once we obtain some transportation, we're going back to see where those trucks ended up."

Jack simply nodded at Mac's plan as they both continued walking down the road.

It was nearly a mile later before Mac finally stopped and pointed to a large residential property that had just a few exterior lights on, and no indication of anyone occupying the home's interior. The entrance was a paved road that ended in a circular drive at the front of the home's entrance. What had caught Mac's attention was the smaller building just adjacent to the main house. His instincts told him that other building might contain a vehicle.

The two men made their way slowly down the property's driveway, keeping to the shadows as they did so. Upon arriving at the smaller building, Mac paused, looking for any signs of a security system. Jack was already doing the same.

"Looks clear Mac – nothing."

Mac was pleased to see three large commercial style exterior doors at the front of the stucco building.

"Sure as hell looks like a place to store some vehicles."

Jack stood in front of what appeared to be the structure's entrance door and found it locked with a single, large deadbolt. Holding the sniper rifle in his hands, Jack looked to Mac and then pointed the end of the rifle at the deadbolt.

"Mind if I do the honors?"

Mac's teeth could be seen flashing faintly in the darkness as he smiled while taking a few steps away from the door.

"By all means Alabama – but try to keep the noise down."

Jack fired just one of the AS-50's armor piercing incendiary explosive rounds into the deadbolt and accompanying door frame, creating a momentary explosion that sent disintegrated bits of metal and stucco flying in all directions. The detonation echoed momentarily across the Benghazi desert before the area returned to silence again.

Jack looked approvingly at the result. Nearly half of the door had been blown from the frame, the remaining half leaning inward by a single hinge. Mac gave a low whistle as he ran a hand along fragments of stucco.

"Son-of-a-bitch do I love fifty caliber firepower."

Both men proceeded slowly inside the building, pausing to allow their eyes time to adjust to the interior darkness. Mac felt Jack tap his shoulder.

"Hey dumbass, use the night vision."

Mac chuckled at the obvious that he had to admit, he hadn't thought of. As they brought the binoculars to their eyes, Jack's enthusiasm made itself known.

"Oh hell yeah."

Two vehicles were parked inside. The first, and not the source of Jack's enthusiasm, was an older Chevy station wagon with wood paneled sides. The second vehicle was a massive, all black 2010 H2 Hummer with darkened windows and a custom, all chrome mesh grill.

Jack ran his right hand along the Hummer while Mac considered the practicality of the station wagon. As Jack caught Mac's indecision, he turned around and pointed dismissively at the Chevy wagon.

"Not that one Mac. We go big or we go home."

Mac shook his head.

"That thing will draw attention to itself Jack. That's the last thing we need."

Jack refused to go along with Mac's suggestion.

"Bullshit. Look at the tinted glass. They can't see inside. Plus, which one of these do you want to be caught in a firefight with Mac? We just look like your typical rich Libyan coming down the street. You want to draw attention to yourself, take out that family truckster and that's what you'll get. I didn't see any of those on the road when we were driving through Benghazi."

Mac knew Jack was likely exaggerating the conspicuousness of the station wagon, but he had a point about the darkened windows and the possibility the Hummer would allow them to pass as a wealthy Libyan and thus, not be bothered as much by the authorities. Also, as much as he hated to admit it, the Hummer was just plain cool.

"Ok Alabama – let's take the damn Hummer."

Jack was already opening the driver door of the monstrous SUV, his hands clapping together as he found the keys already in the ignition, as well as the control unit for the garage door.

"Telling you Mac – it was meant to be man. Meant to be!"

By the time Mac was settling into the passenger seat Jack was already driving the Hummer slowly away from the building, the large access door closing behind them.

"Gonna go dark Mac, no headlights – use the night vision."

It was a good idea, one that Mac again wished he had already thought of. Jack was on his game.

"Take us back to where those transport trucks were heading. See if we can locate their location."

Jack nodded and pushed down on the Hummer's accelerator, grinning as the big V8 Vortec engine rumbled its approval. It took no more than a minute for them to come to the same turn the United Nations trucks had taken. Jack headed down the secondary road, as both he and Mac scanned the area through their night vision binoculars.

"Pull off the road Jack – something headed our way."

Jack had already spotted the same set of headlights Mac was referring to. With the Hummer's headlights still off, he moved the SUV some thirty yards off of the road, its black exterior blending into the dark desert landscape.

Another of the food relief trucks drove past them, coming out of a gate just up the road from where Mac and Jack's location.

"Leave this parked here and let's take a walk. I want to see what that place is. We'll stay off the road, come in from the side where that little hill is over there. That should give us a good vantage point."

Moments later, Mac Walker found himself looking down on a property enclosed by a well built, thick stucco wall, with at least four security personnel walking the perimeter while two more armed men manned the access gate. Unlike the property they were instructed to watch from their safe house, none of the security team appeared to be Libyan. They were all white men. Several buildings were housed inside the property walls. The only vehicles Mac could see were four unmarked black sedans, identical to the one he had seen earlier at the property across the road from the safe house.

Mac felt Jack nudge him. The big man was pointing into the night sky.

"Two hundred yards out, moving directly over the property."

Mac followed where Jack indicated and saw, courtesy of the night vision binoculars, the profile of yet another drone moving silently across the desert no more than fifty yards off the ground. Unlike the earlier drone they had seen before though, this one appeared to be armed.

"We sure as hell aren't the only other ones who know about that place."

Both men watched as the drone flew directly over the heads of the armed security team before it disappeared into the darkness.

"Now I might be a dumb, corn fed redneck Alabama boy, but what the hell would the United Nations need so much security for a place that has a bunch of food relief trucks stopping by?"

Mac gave Jack's question a thin smile, already aware of the implications of the possible answer.

"They ain't moving food. And to be using trucks that big, and all the security involved…"

Mac's comment trailed off as he and Jack continued to peer down into the property. It wasn't the possibility of arms dealing that had Mac unsettled. It was the seeming involvement of the CIA that appeared to be orchestrating the operation - and Mac and his team's still uncertain secondary involvement in whatever that operation was intending. He had no problem pissing off a mob of angry Muslims, but coming in on the wrong side of the CIA was another matter entirely.

First they would return to the safe house and then tomorrow, Mac would drive into Benghazi and get a sit down with Ella and hope she could provide some answers.

XVIII.

Ray Tilley sat in the darkness of his home office, wondering who he could turn to find the answers he promised Mac he would give him. His conversation with Dasha left him more certain than ever that something truly insidious was being undertaken in Benghazi, and Tilley was the one responsible for putting Mac's team in the middle of it.

His cell phone, sitting on his desk, began buzzing. The number displayed indicated it was the general.

"This is Tilley."

"Mr. Tilley, I have some more information for you. Could you possibly stop by my home to see it? Say, first thing in the morning?"

Why is he wanting to see me in person? Is it a trap? Did someone get to the general?

"Mr. Tilley – are you there? Don't keep me waiting on the phone, son."

"I apologize sir. I just…I wasn't expecting your call."

General Vannatter's tone lowered slightly.

"This isn't some kind of trap Mr. Tilley. I just don't want to talk about this stuff over the phone. So will I see you tomorrow morning? You remember the way, right?"

Tilley decided to trust the general.

"Yes sir, I remember. I'll be there."

Ray Tilley awoke just before dawn and prepared for the five hour drive to the general's home in West Virginia. Given the early hour, traffic was still light, allowing Tilley to push the BMW a bit and make good time. He arrived at General Vannatter's spacious country estate shortly after 8:00 a.m.

The house was as Tilley remembered it when he last visited here almost three years ago. That was for the reception that followed the general's funeral for his wife of thirty nine years. She had been suffering from congenital heart failure for nearly a decade and finally collapsed in the bathroom, fell into a coma, and passed away in the intensive care unit of the area hospital four days later. It was the first and only time Ray Tilley had seen the general appear so weak and helpless.

The Vannatter home was a large four bedroom red bricked Tudor-styled home so common to the upper classes in this part of the United States. Tilley recalled the main room with the massive oak beam that ran from one end of the sixteen foot high ceiling to the other, a beam the general had once informed him was put there when the home was originally built in 1887.

Tilley saw the entrance door open and the bent figure of a man he once regarded as among the most intimidating men he had ever known. The last few years had not been kind to the general. He was more frail, and the upper portion of his spine now noticeably forward. When he looked at Tilley and smiled though, the general's hawkish eyes still gleamed with clarity and pride. Though a physical shadow of what he once was, the general's legendary clarity and pride remained within him.

"Mr. Tilley, so glad to see you again."

General Vannatter extended a slightly trembling hand, which Tilley gladly took, noting how thin and fragile the general's skin now felt as he shook it.

"Thank you sir. And thank you for the call. I appreciate all the help I can get on this one."

The general's eyes looked past Tilley, scanning the driveway behind him.

"Come in Mr. Tilley - we need to talk."

Tilley followed the general past the main room, and down a long hallway to where Tilley now remembered the general's study to be. It was a room with its own fireplace, and a large window overlooking the property's horse pastures. The general would spend hours watching his beloved horses moving about the fields.

"Any soldier who isn't a lover of horses is no soldier I want in my command."

Ray Tilley smiled to himself as he recalled those words from the general spoken to him years ago as they both looked out from the same window they now stood in front of.

"Have a seat Mr. Tilley."

Tilley sat across from the general's simple, steel lined Tanker desk – the same one the general had used during his time at the Pentagon.

"Have you heard any more from your. Mr. Mardian?"

Tilley shook his head.

"Well, I did what you asked Mr. Tilley. Asked around a bit about this Dasha Al Marri. Very interesting woman. Very connected. So much so that my initial contact shut me down. Got scared. They didn't want anything to do with looking into her business."

"That normal?"

The general shook his head.

"No, especially not from this person. They've been feeding me information for years. The fact they backed away just made it more interesting, so I made a call into someone I know at Fort Meade. As you might recall, I had Level Three clearance there right up to my retirement, and still have some folks from my era kicking around. Your request begins with this Dasha woman, so that's where I'll start."

Tilley knew the reference to Fort Meade meant N.S.A. The general went to the big time to find more out on Dasha.

"As I said earlier, I knew a bit of her family, her father. She's expanded the family's portfolio quite a bit though. A very political woman, with direct ties to the Saudi Royal Family. My guess, and that is all it is because she's done a hell of a job muddying her own waters, is that she's working for the Saudis. She was educated in London, very familiar with Western culture, attractive, all the elements for a good facilitator."

Tilley raised an eyebrow, confused over the general's choice of word.

"Facilitator?"

General Vannatter smiled warmly back as he took a piece of paper from a simple manila file folder and slid it across his desk toward Tilley.

"Look at those dates in the left column. Do they ring familiar to you in any way Mr. Tilley?"

Tilley shook his head. The dates appeared random. The general continued.

"The first few dates are during the first half of 2009. What are the locations on the right side column that corresponds to those first few dates Mr. Tilley?"

Tilley saw it was Kyrgyzstan.

"Kyrgyzstan."

The general paused to see if Tilley would find any significance. When Tilley remained silent, the general continued.

"In late 2008, Kyrgyzstan completed a rather significant natural gas and oil feasibility study. Those dates in 2009 indicate personal visits this Dasha Al Marri made to Krygystan. Do you recall what happened by late 2009 and early 2010 in Kyrgyzstan, Mr. Tilley?"

Suddenly Ray Tilley grasped the significance.

"Revolution. The government was overthrown. Some of our own Intel people later said that Kyrgyzstan was the real start of the Arab Spring."

General Vannatter pointed a finger at Tilley, as excited for the realization as Tilley was.

"That's right Mr. Tilley. Now if this was a one time deal involving this Dasha, perhaps we could argue coincidence. What are the next two dates in the left column though?"

Tilley scanned the left column.

"They are both in September, 2010. Location is…Tunisia."

Ray Tilley didn't need the general to explain the significance this time – he already knew that within a few months of those dates, Tunisia would be in the grips of a revolution and the government toppled.

"Yes, Tunisia, and just like Kyrgyzstan, Tunisia too has experienced significant growth in its gas and oil explorations. Now go on to the next five dates and corresponding locations Mr. Tilley."

Tilley saw five dates in October and November of 2010. The location was Egypt.

"She was in Egypt too? Right before the revolution there?"

The general nodded back slowly.

"Not only was she there – but we know of at least five times! Now Kyrgyzstan and Tunisia are still minor players on the global energy market scene, though showing potential. Egypt though, well that country offers energy production that can he cashed in for big profits right now. In order to effectively maximize those profits though, would require a bit of a...change in leadership to one more accommodating certain outside interests.

Now look at the last set of dates and locations Mr. Tilley, and tell me what you see."

Ray Tilley looked down and saw three dates in December of 2010 and January of 2011. The location was Libya – Benghazi, Libya. By early 2011, Libyan dictator Muammar Gaddafi would be facing his own revolution. In March of that year, the United Nations enforced a no fly zone over Libya, effectively preventing Gaddafi from defending himself against rebel attack as NATO forces pummeled the Gaddafi regime with Tomahawk missile and drone attacks. By October of that year, Gaddafi would be dead.

Tilley leaned back in the chair across from the general's desk and closed his eyes, focusing on calming his mind so he could think clearly.

"So she uses her United Nations status as a cover to travel to all of these locations?"

General Vannatter nodded.

"That certainly appears to be the case. That's not all though. Just in case there was any remaining doubt what this woman is up to, and who she truly represents, look at this photo."

Tilley recognized the face – it was that of one of Libya's most prominent post-Gaddafi government officials. A man some were indicating would be the country's future prime minister.

'That there is Ali Zubahn. Before the Libyan revolution he was a human rights lawyer who worked primarily with---"

Tilley interrupted the general, something he normally would never do.

"United Nations - they both are linked together at the U.N."

The general didn't seem to mind being cut off, instead nodding his approval at Tilley's comments.

"Exactly. And more than that, Zubahn's primary residence was London. He was educated there – just like this Dasha Al Marri. Now take a look at this copy of an internal communication that comes directly from Zubahn's office to a ranking member of the newly formed Libyan Congress less than a month ago.

Tilley read the brief memo, the words causing his former headache to threaten a sudden return.

August 8th, 2012

Per our earlier discussions, I must maintain my recommendation regarding moving of state owned oil administrations to Benghazi from current location in Tripoli as soon as possible. This move will facilitate much needed job creation in that region and bring it further stabilization. Libya must now move back into the fold of the Arab world and put an end to the former power's ill advised and arrogant pro-African slant. I believe such a move will also enhance improvements in our relations with fellow OPEC nations, most importantly Saudi Arabia.

This is also an essential moment for Libya to rejoin the world community. In the coming months, I intend to work closely with our affiliates at the United Nations. I am very hopeful of that organization's own current transformations into a new era, a new United Nations if you will.

Regards,

Ali Zubahn

Member,

National Party for Development and Welfare

Tilley placed the memo back onto the general's desk. The situation in Benghazi, though still riddled with questions, was becoming somewhat more clear. Dasha represented Saudi oil interests – interests that now appeared intent on securing a great share of Libya's oil production. The same interests who did the same throughout the region, toppling one government and replacing it with another that would be more favorable to the Saudi's influence. The reference to a "new" United Nations was certainly not lost on Tilley either. It seemed that term was quickly gaining in popularity.

'That's not quite the last of it Mr. Tilley. Something else was given to me - something particularly troubling given your men's current location in Benghazi. I have another photo for you."

Tilley looked at a picture of a lean faced man in his mid fifties, with grey streaked hair combed back from his forehead. The face was unfamiliar to him.

"Who's this?"

The general smiled slightly, though is eyes held no humor in them.

"That is the current head of the U.N. humanitarian operations in Benghazi. He works out of the Benini airport, so has access to everything coming and going from there, and right now, there's a whole hell of a lot coming and going in and out of Benghazi. His name is Louis Danton. Been with the United Nations for almost thirty years and it's a rather interesting resume. This is not the first time he's been assigned to Libya."

Tilley could sense his apprehension growing within him.

"This Danton – when was he there before?"

General Vannatter cleared his throat as he leaned toward Tilley.

"He was there a decade ago Mr. Tilley, as part of a United Nations assessment team. They were investigating Gaddafi's abandoned nuclear arms program. Now I personally know that while Gaddafi may have been some years away from developing a fully viable nuclear weapon, his government did secure amounts of radiological fissile materials. To my knowledge, those materials have never been fully accounted for."

Ray Tilley took a deep breath.

"General, are you suggesting that some of the arms dealing my team was sent to do surveillance on could include nuclear materials?"

The general's eyebrows raised slightly as he looked back at Tilley.

"Yes, I would certainly be willing to entertain that possibility. What better opportunity to disperse that kind of material than during the ongoing chaos that is currently Libya? And who better to do it than people with United Nations clearance? And I'll take it a step further now Mr. Tilley. Let's talk motivation. Base that motivation on previous examples. This Dasha Al Mari goes into a country a number of times, and then months later, that country's government is overthrown. Mass chaos, bloodshed, and then it's replaced by a new regime all while subjecting itself to increased United Nations involvement. What if this whole Arab Spring thing is them preparing the runway for the big show? The real purpose behind all of this?

What if, Mr. Tilley, your men in Benghazi, now find themselves at Ground Zero of some kind of global restructuring? The very same kind of restructuring that has taken place recently throughout other parts of the world? I know you caught the last part of that communication from Ali Zubahn. He called it a "new" United Nations, right? That sounds rather ominous to me Mr. Tilley. How about you? Now please take a look at this last bit of information I have for you today. It is a single date and location.

Tilley looked at the paper. Like the earlier example, it too was divided by a column on the left with a date, and a column on the right with a corresponding location. This one indicated September 6th, 2012. Yesterday - the very day he had sat in the back of Dasha Al Mari's car after having been followed by Nigel. The location caused Tilley to inhale sharply as he felt a layer of sweat forming on his forehead. For a brief moment he thought he might be sick.

The location was the White House.

XIX.

Three hours after Ray Tilley had left his home to return to Washington D.C., General Vannatter found himself feeling very tired. It seems he was always feeling tired these days, especially being alone in his big, West Virginia home he had intended to live out his days with his wife Elizabeth. She had unwillingly left him to fend for himself though, finally succumbing to the weak heart that had plagued her last years of life.

Despite the fatigue, the general had enjoyed the morning's conversation with Mr. Tilley – enjoyed it immensely in fact. He almost felt like his old self. Almost. The morning coffee had worn off though, so now it was time for some noon hour tea. He moved slowly, being particularly careful with filling the tea kettle. The shaking of his hands had grown worse in recent months. Doctors informed him two years ago it was Parkinson's. His children had wanted him to sell the house, saying he shouldn't be alone. To hell with all that. He'd be dying in this house thank you very much, and the Parkinson's could just kiss his tired old military four star ass.

Having put the tea on, General Vannatter settled into one of the two chairs at the kitchen table and looked out the small window that faced the home's driveway. That's when he saw the unmarked black sedan slowly drive up and park just outside the front door.

I'll be damned, they actually sent someone after me. Guess they still consider me some kind of threat. Likely an easy target too.

The thought made the general smile. Now he really was feeling like his old self. He rose from his chair and turned the burner down and then checked inside the cupboard just above the stove before turning back around and making his way to the front door. Halfway there he heard the doorbell ring once, and then ring again.

I'm coming, you traitorous, murdering bastard. I know your kind all too well. Used to send them off to all corners of the world myself, back in the day.

The general unlocked the front door and opened it, trying to appear surprised at the visit from the tall, dark suited man standing at the entrance to his home. The agent was in his mid-forties, with eyes that held no emotion, his cleanly shaven face equally unreadable.

"Hello General Vannatter, I'm Agent Bronson, Homeland Security. I was hoping to speak with you for a few minutes about a guest you had at your home earlier today."

The man's voice was flat, nondescript, the introduction well rehearsed. The general knew at that moment the agent intended to kill him.

Get him into the house you old fool, so you have a chance of giving as good as you get.. Die like a proper soldier dammit!

"Oh – ok. Come on in then, I've got the stove on…need to turn it off if that's ok."

The agent nodded, moving toward the entrance as he glanced back toward his car and the long driveway behind him.

Get your ass in here you killing bastard. See what I've got for you.

The general stood up straight and placed his right hand against the agent's chest.

"Hold on, you said you were with Homeland Security, is that right?"

The agent again nodded, his eyes flashing brief annoyance at the general's hand pushing against his chest.

"Yes sir. Here's my identification."

The agent held up the standard, government issued Homeland Security credentials.

"Thank you. Please, come on in then. Sorry to have asked but you know, these days, you just never know."

The agent managed a strained smile.

"Of course sir."

"Right this way then, the kitchen is down the hall here. We can talk in there if that's ok."

The agent replied as he followed closely behind General Vannatter.

"That's fine, whatever is most comfortable for you."

Once inside the kitchen, the general motioned for the agent to have a seat at the table while he moved to the stove and turned it off.

"I'm making some tea, would you like some agent Bronson? It's Earl Grey."

"No thank you sir. Can you tell me who you spoke with this morning General Vannatter?"

The general paused as he reached into the cupboard above the stove.

"Oh, an old friend of mine. A former staffer from my Pentagon days."

The general sensed the agent tensing inside the kitchen, preparing to strike.

And this friend of yours, can you confirm his name was a Mr. Ray Tilley?"

General Vannatter turned around to look back at the agent, his face revealing a seemingly harmless smile before he turned back toward the stove.

"Yes, yes it was. Can you tell me what this is about Agent Bronson?"

The general heard the agent rising slowly from the chair to his feet. He was trying to be quiet, but in a man's own house, you become very familiar with how things should sound and feel.

General Vannatter had not shot at another human being in many-many years, but perhaps experience with such things was much like riding a bike. It was just something one never truly forgot how to do. The general realized in that brief moment, and with great satisfaction, that his hand was no longer trembling.

Agent Bronson's eyes grew wide as he saw the general's handgun pointed at him. Bronson had already drawn his own weapon. Both men fired at the same time.

General Martin Vannatter felt the immense pressure of the bullet hit him in the middle of his chest, the force throwing his body back up against the stove, spilling the hot contents of the tea kettle onto the kitchen floor.

Nice shot Agent Bronson. You showed some poise there even when I surprised you with my own weapon. You would have made a good soldier.

The general's lungs were already filling with blood as his body slid down the front of the stove, his knees buckling beneath him.

Did I kill him? Please God, let me have done it right.

Whether or not God approved of the general's actions was uncertain, but given the result, the general had certainly done it right. A single bullet hole marked its entrance in the middle of Agent Bronson's forehead, killing him instantly. The general had correctly guessed Agent Bronson was wearing a protective Kevlar vest, and so, had aimed for the agent's head. Able to see he had in fact killed the man sent to kill him, the general devoted his energies to standing back up onto his feet and making his way to his study on the other side of the house. The task took nearly ten minutes, the general's breathing becoming more labored, his legs increasingly weak. By the time he slumped into his study chair behind his desk, he was coughing up significant amounts of his own blood.

General Vannatter slowly turned the chair to face the window looking outside to the pastures so he could watch his beloved horses. As luck would have it, all three were gathered in front of the window, seemingly looking back at the dying general.

Got to go out like a soldier, and do it in my own home. Not such a bad day after all…

XX.

Ray Tilley needed a drink. Hell, he needed a dozen drinks. With Mac and the team trapped in Benghazi, with Mardian refusing to give either help or real answers, and now the knowledge that the assignment was likely always intended to have been a kill mission against Americans, it all left Tilley with a terrible headache and far too much uncertainty about what to do next.

We are so fucked.

That thought kept running itself through Tilley's head, and now as he sat on a bar stool inside some hole in the wall roadside bar just outside of Washington D.C., Tilley knew it was likely to get worse with less chance of ever getting better. He had not done his due diligence, and Mac, Benny, Minnick, and Jack were all paying the price for his stupidity in trusting Mardian and Dasha Al Marri.

"What can I get you boss?"

The man behind the bar had the look of one who had lived a life that had taken much and given back little. Nearing sixty, with long lanky grey hair and a deeply lined, almost gaunt face, the bartender had most certainly seen countless examples of men at the end of their rope stumbling into this bar looking for alcohol's promise of temporary respite.

Guys like me who know too damn much but can't do shit about it.

Tilley gave the bartender a half smile and muttered back his order.

"Whiskey – no ice."

The bartender paused.

"Got a preference boss?"

Tilley shrugged.

"Whatever you prefer. Just keep it coming."

The man offered Tilley a knowing nod of the head as he placed a shot glass and began pouring from a bottle of Wild Turkey.

"Ah, one of those days huh?"

Ray Tilley placed the shot glass to his lips and emptied the contents, feeling the warmth of the liquid light a small fire inside of his throat.

"You could say so. This world is in one hell of a mess, and I'm about done with it. Give me another one."

The bartender refilled Tilley's shot glass and watched as Tilley emptied it.

"Oh, nothing can be all that bad can it?"

Ray Tilley closed his eyes and took a deep breath, trying again to force his mind to come up with a viable plan to get Mac and his team back safely to the United States.

You really think any of you are safe here? You're probably in almost as much danger as they are.

Tilley opened his eyes and nodded back at the bartender.

"Another one."

Before Tilley could put the shot glass to his lips for a third time, he caught an image of a familiar face flash across the flat screen TV that hung from the right corner of the bar.

It was the face of General Vannatter – the man whose house Tilley had left not more than five hours ago. A dull pain began to knot deep in Tilley's stomach.

"Can you turn that up?"

The bartender turned to locate the remote, slowly moving the volume up so the news report could be heard over the din of the inhabitants of the small bar.

"General Martin Vannatter was found dead in his West Virginia home this afternoon, the victim of what authorities are describing as an apparent robbery. General Vannatter was a highly decorated member of the U.S. Military, and in the final years of his career, a well regarded fixture at the Pentagon. General Vannatter retired from the military a decade ago. Pentagon officials have already released a statement indicating their sorrow at hearing of the general's death, indicating he was a fine solider, and an even better man."

He was killed for talking to me. Who would do that? Mardian? Dasha? The fucking White House?

Tilley's phone rang. He had forgotten he left it on. It was Mardian.

He wants to know where I'm at, so he can kill me too. I got to call Mac, let him know what the general told me. Let him know he's on his own...

Tilley stood up from his bar stool and began walking toward the exit door.

"Hey boss – you gonna pay me for the shots?"

Tilley turned back around as he reached into his pocket and withdrew a twenty dollar bill, which he then placed gently onto the counter.

"Sorry about that."

The bartender smiled back as his eyes glanced behind Tilley.

"Hey, a little heads up for you boss. Guy came in a few minutes ago, sitting in the back left corner of the room. Hasn't taken his eyes off you since he came in. When you're phone rang, his eyes were burning a hole in your back."

Ray Tilley stood at the bar counter, forcing himself to focus fully on getting himself out of the bar and away from whoever it was who appeared to be following him. The call from Mardian was likely a way for the man to confirm who Tilley was. Now it was only a matter of time before that man made his move.

So you gotta move first.

"You have a back exit?"

The bartender nodded.

"Sure – hallway to your left, past the restroom. The door says an alarm will sound, but it won't. Been broke for years."

Tilley nodded and then moved quickly toward the hallway, running past the restroom before pushing the rear exit door open and emerging into a small alleyway in the back of the bar. It was still daylight outside, allowing Tilley to see if anyone was watching him from the alley. He appeared to be alone – for now.

A large dumpster sat to the right of the exit door. It had wheels, allowing Tilley to push it in front of the door. A few seconds after doing so, Tilley felt the door bang against the dumpster as the man who had been watching him from inside the bar attempted to get outside as well.

The man yelled out from behind the door.

"Mr. Tilley – I'm with Mardian! I'm supposed to help you!"

Tilley was about to run down the alleyway in an attempt to make it to his car, but paused after hearing the man's claim.

"How the hell you find me here? You been tailing me all day?"

The man pushed the door open a few inches more.

"Yeah. Mardian said you were in danger. I've been watching you since you left his office yesterday. Please Mr. Tilley, I'm just trying to do my job. I'm just trying to protect you."

That means he knows of your meeting with the general.

Tilley took out his phone and called Stephen Mardian. Mardian picked up on the first ring.

"About time you called me back asshole. Where you been?"

Tilley moved away from the blocked door and whispered back to Mardian.

"Did you send someone to follow me Mardian? I need an answer right now."

Mardian paused on the other end before he spoke very slowly, but very deliberately back to Tilley.

"Ray, if there's someone after you, they didn't come from me. Get the hell out of there. Wherever you are, fucking run Ray. Right now."

Tilley hung up as the man behind the door managed to push it open nearly a foot.

"Were you talking to someone Mr. Tilley? Can you please help to open the door?"

Ray Tilley was already gone from the alleyway, moving quickly to the front of the building where his BMW was parked. As he hit the ignition button Tilley caught sight of a man emerging from the bar's front entrance. He was of average height and build, with darkish skin and darker hair – possibly Middle Eastern. The man glared back at Tilley through the windshield as his right hand moved to the inside of his cream colored summer jacket.

He's gonna shoot my ass dead right here in the parking lot.

Tilley slammed the BMW into reverse as a single bullet hole ripped through the right side of the windshield. The gun had made almost no sound when it fired, indicating the man was using a silencer.

The man moved smoothly toward the front of the BMW as it backed into the street, firing off another round that ripped another small hole through the windshield and moved just inches past the right side of Tilley's face, causing him to flinch and move his body against the driver's door.

What the hell would Mac Walker do in a situation like this?

The thought made Tilley smile. He wasn't sure why it popped into his head, but it made him pause inside of the BMW as he watched the man continue to move forward with his gun raised, preparing to fire yet another round at him.

Tilley moved the BMW into drive and mashed his foot down onto the accelerator. The car's twin turbocharged V8 pulled Tilley back into the seat as the car lunged forward toward the armed man, whose eyes grew wide as his mouth dropped open in shock. He managed to fire his weapon one last time, though the bullet glanced off the BMW's right pillar as the car's hood struck the man's upper legs and groin, sending him flying back against the outer wall of the bar. The man's head slammed into the building's exterior with a sickening wet crunching smack before his body crumpled onto the paved entrance.

That's what Mac Walker would have done.

Ray Tilley backed his car onto the road and sped off as people began to emerge from the bar wondering what the loud thud was that was both heard and felt from inside.

Call Mac and get to Mardian's.

Tilley was smiling again. He still didn't know how he would get Mac and the team out of Benghazi, he didn't know who killed the general, didn't know if Mardian could be trusted, and didn't know who was trying to kill him, but he had a plan, however short term, and that sure as hell made him feel better.

For now…

XXI.

Mac Walker looked back at his men as they sat in the early morning darkness of their Benghazi safe house. They had made certain to not use any of the interior lights, wanting the place to appear vacant to anyone passing by. Even the just stolen Hummer parked outside was well hidden under a low hanging palm tree on the side of the large two story house.

"Jack and me are going into Benghazi to meet up with Ella at her office. At least, we're gonna try. Minnick and Benny, you two are to stay here and continue doing surveillance on the house across the road. Not really sure who we trust to report to at this point, but I still want an idea of who and what is coming and going from over there."

The features of Benny's dark skinned face were difficult to make out in the gloom of the home's main room as he asked Mac about contacting Tilley.

"What about Tilley – he's supposed to get back to you, right?"

Mac nodded, but his face betrayed his uncertainty over any information coming from Ray Tilley.

"Yeah, that's what he said, but it's been a while now and not a word back from him. Don't know why the delay, but until I hear back, I'm gonna try to get some answers on my own, and that Ella woman is the only one I can think of around here who might have them, and be willing to speak with us."

"Don't forget Mac, she was sent our way by Tilley. If you can't trust him, you might not be able to trust her."

Mac had already considered what Minnick pointed out, but at this point, he had decided they didn't have a choice. Plus, his instincts told him she could be trusted, and to this point, it was instinct that had kept him alive in this business.

Jack was already making his way to the door as Mac followed behind him. Both men were again carrying one of the fifty caliber sniper rifles that had been left for them at the safe house, and two additional boxes of ammo. Mac paused to speak briefly to Benny and Minnick before closing the door behind him.

"Lay low gentleman. We should be back this time tomorrow, hopefully with some idea of where we go from here."

Minutes later, with Jack behind the wheel, the black Hummer H2 was travelling toward the main area of Benghazi at nearly eighty miles an hour.

"You in a hurry Alabama?"

Jack's eyes were focused on the quickly passing road in front of him as he looked through the night vision binoculars that allowed him to drive without the headlights on.

"If we can get there before daylight, seems like the way to go."

Mac nodded. Jack was right – cover of darkness was always a preferred mode of transportation.

Soon they were parking the Hummer a block from Ella's office building. Both men moved as quietly as possible from the SUV and began making their way down the road, Jack looking ahead as Mac kept watch for anything behind them. Sunlight was now peeking out from behind some of the taller Benghazi buildings. The city would be waking up soon.

Mac and Jack stood outside the entrance to Ella's building, trying to determine if anyone was inside.

"What the hell are you two doing here?"

Mac whirled around with the fifty caliber rifle pointed out in front of him. Behind him and Jack stood Udi, the one Ella had drive them to the safe house the other day. He was holding his own handgun, though as soon as he recognized it was Mac and Jack, lowered it.

Mac lowered his rifle as well.

"I need to speak to Ella."

Udi glanced at Jack and then back to Mac.

"She's in a meeting right now. I thought she told you not to contact her again."

Mac nodded.

"Yeah – she did. Our situation has become…more challenging than we anticipated. I need her help Udi. I'm hoping she has some answers for me."

Udi's eyes scanned the street.

"You do a better job of not being followed this time, or did you bring the mob with you again?"

Jack stepped toward Udi, the big man looking down at the Israeli.

"We're good, but I think it'd be better if we get inside."

Udi offered Jack a dismissive smirk as he turned toward the steel framed entrance door.

"C'mon."

Mac and Jack followed Udi past both security doors and into the building, Mac finding himself in the same reception area he had stood in just days earlier.

"Take a seat – wait here."

Jack appeared ready to say something back at Udi, clearly not appreciative of the Israeli's dismissive tone, but a look from Mac caused the big man to hold his tongue.

The two sat down in one of the art deco chairs that sat against the wall of the reception room, waiting for Udi's return. Jack was looking around the room, trying to figure out what the place actually was.

"The sign outside says this place is a media center? I don't think so. They Israeli intelligence? Private contractors like us?"

Mac looked over at Jack and then leaned his head back against the reception room wall.

"Something like that. Tilley vouched for them, which is pretty much all I know. Not that that means shit to us anymore. They are well trained, well armed, and seem to know how to handle themselves, so hopefully they'll be on our side. We could use the help about now."

Mac turned his head to the right as he heard footsteps approaching from the hallway that Mac already knew led to a conference room. It was Udi.

"Mr. Walker, please follow me."

As Jack rose from his own seat, Udi pointed back down at him.

"Not you – just Mr. Walker."

Jack wasn't pleased, and let the Israeli know it.

"Bullshit. I'd like to see you try and stop me."

Udi's eyes flashed momentarily, showing no fear in the prospect of taking on Jack. Mac turned to the Alabama native and gently pushed him back down into his seat.

"It's ok Jack, keep an eye on the door. We're guests here, and we arrived unannounced, remember?"

Jack glared back at Udi, his jaw clenching in fury.

"Yeah – got it."

Udi turned and began walking back toward the hallway as Mac followed him to the conference room door.

"Right in there Mr. Walker, Ella will see you now. Please try and keep it brief, she is very busy today."

Mac pushed open the conference room door and saw Ella seated at one end of the table, and to her left sat a thin, blonde haired man of perhaps fifty years of age. He wore a navy blue dress shirt with the sleeves rolled up, and tan khaki pants. Both he and Ella stood up from their seats as Mac walked in.

"Mr. Walker, oddly enough, I am not surprised to see you here again, despite my demand that you not do so."

Mac offered Ella a strained, apologetic smile as he took her in again. She struck him as even more attractive than before. Her blonde hair was again pulled neatly back in a bun behind her head, her lithe body clothed in a form fitting black turtleneck sweater and matching black dress pants, a small handgun holstered on her right hip.

"Don't stand there mute Mr. Walker, take a seat. I would like to introduce you to my guest – the American Ambassador to Libya."

Mac tried hard to conceal his shock at the title Ella gave to the man who reached a hand across the table to shake his own.

Did she say this guy was the ambassador?

The man was a couple inches shorter than Mac, and several pounds lighter. His grip was firm though, and his eyes indicated someone who knew risk and challenge, and to this point, had come out ahead more often than not.

"Nice to meet you Mr. Walker. Ella had already mentioned your earlier visit here to me. I am glad to see you are still alive and well. Libya, as you know, is a very dangerous place, and not so forgiving of Americans."

"Or Jews."

Ella made her remark as Mac sat slowly down in his seat, his mind still trying to grasp the presence of the ambassador sitting across the table from him.

"I can see you are trying to figure out what the hell I'm doing here this early in the morning having a meeting with Ms. Lerner. She's been one of my most trusted, off the record contacts here in Benghazi. The Israeli's have an understandable interest in events in this area, and I have been doing my best to keep them updated through, shall we say... unofficial channels."

Mac looked over at Ella, who he caught staring back at him.

"And you would be one of those unofficial channels?"

Ella raised her eyebrows slightly and nodded.

"Well, I have some questions. We were sent here to do surveillance on a house that has trucks pulling in and out of there at all hours of the day and night, and more than a few State Department vehicles too. You know anything about that Mr. Ambassador?"

The ambassador smiled as he folded his hands in front of him.

"Yes, I most certainly do Mr. Walker. That is why I am here, and that in turn is why you're here."

Mac sensed he was about to be told something dramatic. The air felt heavier, and he could see Ella's eyes focus on him with even more intensity than before.

"I'm here because of those trucks? That house? They're running weapons, right?"

The ambassador's friendly demeanor continued, though like Ella, his eyes were now sharper, more focused back at Mac.

"Weapons? Yes – they're running weapons. A lot of weapons Mr. Walker, but that's not why you were sent here. Not really."

Mac found himself leaning toward the ambassador without thinking to do so.

"If it's not because of the weapons, why am I really here Mr. Ambassador?"

The ambassador's eyes were unblinking as he responded.

"You were sent here to kill me, Mr. Walker."

XXII.

Mac felt his phone buzzing from inside one of his jacket pockets. He held up his hand to both Ella and the ambassador as he looked down to see the call was coming from Tilley.

"I need to take this – it's Tilley."

Mac noted the ambassador's eyes didn't change when he heard mention of Ray Tilley, telling Mac the ambassador likely already knew who Tilley was.

"This is Mac – go ahead."

The tone of Tilley's voice told Mac the man was stressed. Big time.

"Mac! I'm drowning in shit on my end. I'll handle me, but…but I don't know how we're going to get you out of there. It's all gone to hell, the whole fucking assignment. It isn't what they said Mac. They want you to kill Americans, and I don't think they ever intended to have you or your men make it back. This thing involves, shit Mac, it involves some very big players. We can't trust anyone on this. Don't know if Mardian was involved or not…I'm on my way to see him now. You have to get out of there Mac…do you understand? Abort the whole fucking assignment and find a way to get the hell out of there."

Mac glanced up to see Ella and the ambassador watching him closely, possibly trying to catch some of Tilley's words.

"Ray, we're ok here for now. No immediate danger. Understand? I'll get us home safely. You need to calm down. Hold your shit together."

Tilley took a deep breath. Mac could tell he was driving as he spoke with him.

"How are you getting out of there Mac? I wouldn't trust the airport. And it's a hell of a long drive from Benghazi to somewhere else."

"Don't have those answers yet Tilley, and even if I did, I wouldn't be telling them to you."

Tilley paused on the other end, likely realizing Mac's continued uncertainty over whether or not he could truly be trusted.

"Understood Mac. Let me know if I can be of help though. Perhaps you can try Ella. She might be able to get you passage out of there."

Mac caught Ella's faint smile. She had heard her name being mentioned by Tilley.

"Don't worry about me right now Tilley. Sounds like you have your hands full. Like I said, hold your shit together."

Tilley hung up as Mac returned his phone to his pocket and looked back at the ambassador and Ella. The ambassador was the first to respond.

"Your Mr. Tilley – he's the one who coordinates the assignments for you, correct?"

Mac sensed the ambassador was letting him know he knew at least some of what Mac and his team did for a living.

"Did Ella fill you in on that? What I do?"

The ambassador's smile returned as his eyes continued to stare into Mac.

"No Mr. Walker, I knew of your assignment here several days ago. You see, I, like so many others now here in Libya, am more than the title would suggest."

"You're CIA."

The ambassador's eyes betrayed no surprise at Mac's statement.

"Yes, I am. The CIA currently has a very significant presence in Libya, and Benghazi is the focal point for that presence."

Mac glanced at Ella, who sat motionless at the head of the table. Her face remained unreadable.

"I have questions Mr. Ambassador. Do you have the answers?"

"I will do my best Mr. Walker, though I don't have much time left to do so here. I must travel back to Tripoli soon."

Mac Walker wasn't yet certain if the ambassador would tell him the truth, but he also knew he and his men had little choice at this point. They needed answers if they were going to have a chance of returning home alive.

"Why am I supposed to kill you?"

The ambassador chuckled.

"Right to the point – I like that Mr. Walker. You were sent here to kill me because I've become something of a liability to certain groups who intend to use the recent and quite dangerous chaos of the Middle East and North Africa and shall we say, extend its boundaries elsewhere. I take issue with that plan, and intend to intervene. That intervention is now the motivation for some to see me dead. And I assure you Mr. Walker, you are likely but one of several options to see that task done."

Mac decided to push ahead with as many questions as he could ask within whatever time the ambassador was to remain at Ella's office. He would have to decide later if how much, if any, of the answers were truthful.

"Do you know who Mark Densmore is?"

The ambassador nodded back.

"Yes. He is among those who want me dead Mr. Walker. He is the direct contact for the Attorney General. Mr. Densmore answers to him. He is responsible for making certain I don't interfere with the arms deals."

"So why doesn't Densmore just kill you himself?"

The ambassador nodded slightly, seeming to approve of the manner in which Mac was asking his questions.

"Too much risk to him, and to the administration itself. I'm certain he would, and will try, if it comes to that. Right now though, you and your men are to take care of it. Very soon Mr. Walker, you will receive that message. I am certain of it. They will paint me as a criminal, a radicalized rogue working to arm the insurgents of Libya. As is so often the case with these kinds of people, you simply find the truth among the accusations they make against those they deem their enemies."

Mac crossed his arms across his chest, his instincts telling him the ambassador truly believed what he was telling him.

"Are you arming the insurgents?"

The ambassador shook his head.

"No…not me. I knew of it of course, but for the most part, was keeping myself out of the way. Gunrunning is nothing new for the U.S. government, or any government for that matter. What caused my intervention was the discovery of a very particular kind of weapon they intend to distribute. There is a line I will not cross Mr. Walker, and Benghazi, for me, is now that line."

"And just what is that line Mr. Ambassador? Is it a weapon?"

Ella held up her hand, indicating she wanted to speak. The ambassador nodded his head, deferring to her.

"I assume you're familiar with the term "RDD" Mr. Walker?"

Mac knew the acronym well – radioactive dispersal device. A dirty bomb, something terrorist groups had been working for years to obtain and use.

"Yeah, it's a dirty bomb. Are you saying that's what is going on here in Benghazi? Someone is trying to get their hands on one of those?"

Ella, her face still unreadable, continued.

"Yes, there is at least one we know of. It's presence in Benghazi has been confirmed. It is being held at a CIA facility no more than two miles from your own safe house Mr. Walker. More concerning than that is information indicating at least a dozen more are now on their way to that same facility – they may in fact have already been delivered. They are being kept in containers made to look like simple coffee canisters, using a material known as Strontium-90, a low grade radioactive byproduct."

For the first time since he sat down with the ambassador and Ella, Mac felt a twinge of creeping panic. Guns, even surface to air missiles were one thing, but a radioactive explosive device was something even Mac Walker considered an entirely new level of serious. In the wrong hands, such devices could create the kind of panic and fear in people that outright chaos and destructive mayhem would inevitably follow - the kind of chaos that gave justification for a governmental police state.

"Are you telling me that the United States government is personally involved in disseminating over a dozen or more RDDs to terrorist groups?"

Both Ella and the ambassador remained momentarily silent before the ambassador shifted forward in his seat and again nodded his head.

"In essence – yes Mr. Walker. The gunrunning that you were told to monitor upon your arrival here in Benghazi, is a ruse. That is a cover, a distraction if you will. The real purpose of what is being attempted here in Libya, is, just as you said, the distribution of radioactive weaponry to groups more than willing to use them throughout the world. I'm not saying the entire American government is involved, not by a long shot. But enough of the government, and at positions of great authority, are indeed attempting to do this. Ella's own work here in Benghazi has confirmed for me what I suspected. It is now my duty to try and stop them from succeeding. I intend to shut the operation down very soon. In fact, I have already informed a high ranking official within the Turkish government, who is deeply involved in the operation, of my intentions. And some CIA operatives already here, who I trust, have been informed as well. Others among the CIA, are themselves involved directly. They are likely at present, our greatest threat, both to me, and to you Mr. Walker, and certainly to Ella here as well."

Mac looked at Ella, his eyes seeking some measure of emotion from her. He still found none.

"And what's your stake in this Ella? Why put yourself into this kind of risk?"

Ella Lerner's face finally revealed emotion, a mixture of determination and dangerous intent.

"Survival Mr. Walker – the survival of my country, my people, my family. Who do you think is the primary target of these terrorist groups? It is Israel – it is always Israel. And after Israel, it will be your country next. America is certain to be dealt the catastrophe these Islamists have dreamed for so long to deliver. They intend it to be a death blow Mr. Walker, the end of the United States as you have known it. The time of the Islamic radicals and their cousins the United Nations globalists, has arrived. The two have become one, and freedom and liberty will not be allowed to survive their union."

Mac couldn't hide his shock at the vastness of the plot Ella and the ambassador were laying out before him.

"So what about Louis Danton? I was given that name by Angelo Moretti, the guy who organized our flight into Benghazi. He tried to have me and my team killed the night we arrived. Moretti told me before he died to contact Danton if anything went wrong with the assignment. Danton's United Nations, so I assumed he couldn't be trusted. Is he the one facilitating the movement of these dirty bombs? And if he is, why don't I just go kill him?"

For the first time since sitting down, the ambassador's eyes betrayed, however briefly, a moment of alarm.

"No Mr. Walker, Louis Danton is one of ours. Not directly, but certainly one of us."

Mac's brow furrowed. The ambassador's words made no sense.

"How can Danton be, as you put it, one of ours? His man Moretti tried to have me and my team killed."

The ambassador had already regained his composure, his eyes once again appearing calm, almost amused.

"Mr. Danton has been at this for some time now Mr. Walker. I assure you, if he wanted you or I dead, it would have happened already. Moretti was acting on his own. He has been working with the local militants for some time, and being paid well for it. His turn on you cost him his life of course, so thank you for eliminating what was becoming a problem for all those of us here not on the payroll of the Saudis, or the globalist United Nations operatives. Louis Danton had nothing to do with the attempt on your life. As I said, if he wanted you dead, you most likely would be already."

Mac glanced over at Ella for confirmation of what the ambassador was saying. She simply nodded her head once, but said nothing.

"What about Dasha Al Marri? She was the one calling the shots when I met with her and Tilley and Mardian before coming to Benghazi. What do you know about her Mr. Ambassador?"

The ambassador closed his eyes momentarily before opening them again to look back at Mac.

"She is a very dangerous woman Mr. Walker. As anti-American as you will ever find, extremely well funded, and has an open door to the current administration. She was the one who had you sent here to kill me. She's a globalist, an extremist, and more than willing to kill whoever gets in her way. I happen to be one of those people."

Mac realized then, he had been forced into a corner as soon as he accepted the assignment.

"And me and my team will be one of those people too if we don't kill you, isn't that right?"

The ambassador's smile and sadness over Mac's realization of the position he had been placed in, appeared genuine.

"Yes Mr. Walker, unfortunately, you either kill me, or join me on the hit list. I'm afraid that is your dilemma."

Ella waived a dismissive hand in response to the ambassador's words.

"They will try to kill him either way. Mac, you kill the ambassador and they kill you and your team to make certain none of you can communicate the details of the assignment. You refuse to kill the ambassador, and they still have you all killed for the very same reason."

Mac thought Ella's words over briefly and then nodded. He also noted Ella had, for the first time, addressed him by his first name.

"Ok then, that makes things much simpler. I kill all of them before they kill any of us."

The ambassador laughed as he shook his head.

"If only it were that simple Mr. Walker."

Mac stared back into the ambassador's eyes and smiled, his voice a low growl.

"For me, it really is that simple."

XXIII.

Tilley attempted to reach Mardian for the third time in ten minutes. Finally Mardian picked up, though he remained silent on the other end.

"Mardian? You there?"

The call had gone through, someone had picked up, but whoever it was refused to answer. Tilley ended the call and slowed his car down, not wanting to get too close to Mardian's building at 19th and G. If someone had gotten to Mardian, they were likely waiting for Tilley to make his way back there.

"Shit! Shit! Shit!"

Tilley hoped yelling out his frustration from inside his car would make him feel better.

It didn't.

He couldn't go home. He couldn't go to Mardian's. The general was dead. Tilley's world was closing in on him fast, and if he didn't come up with a plan soon, there'd be no escape from whoever wanted him dead.

The car moved quickly back onto the street as Tilley repeatedly glanced into his rear view mirror.

Need to find a place with lots of people, lots of security.

Tilley moved the big BMW down G Street, past the massive IMF and World Bank buildings toward 17th, which ran parallel to the White House grounds. 17th was busy as always, slowing Tilley's progress. Again he looked behind him, but found no indication he was being followed.

Finally 17th met up with H Street. Tilley moved the car into the far right lane and slammed down on the accelerator for several hundred yards before again turning sharply to the right, bringing him to the entrance of the very popular and much visited, Lafayette Square. Tilley could see several people moving within the meticulously manicured park that faced the front of the White House, the two areas separated by Pennsylvania Avenue.

Tilley opened the glove box and removed the small handgun he kept there. The carrying of handguns in Washington D.C. was forbidden. Even obtaining a license to own a handgun to keep at home, had become increasingly prohibitive in recent years. Taking one into a public park so close to the White House was probably breaking a myriad of local and federal laws Tilley wasn't even aware of.

Not even bothering to see if he was leaving his BMW in an approved parking space, Tilley moved swiftly into Lafayette Square, the bottoms of his heeled shoes echoing off of the red bricked walkway that led to the center of the seven acre park. The leaves of some of the trees were already turning various shades of fall colors, and the air, though still somewhat warm, whispered of the cooler temperatures soon to come as September worked its way inevitably toward October.

There's a bench – a good place to watch anyone coming at me.

Tilley sat down on one of the multiple park benches placed throughout Lafayette Square. This particular one allowed him to put his back against a stone wall, meaning nobody could sneak up on him from behind. In front of him was a group of Japanese tourists, a young couple jogging, and an older man walking his dog. For now, he appeared to be safe.

Should have parked the car several blocks away and walked here. If anyone spots the car, they'll know I'm in the park.

A wave of momentary panic shot through Tilley's mind. Leaving the BMW near the park entrance was a mistake. He wasn't thinking as clearly as he needed to, and that could cost him. His hand, resting inside the right pocket of his jacket, gripped the handgun. The hard steel outline of the weapon brought some measure of reassurance to Tilley as his eyes continued to scan the landscape in front of him.

Ray Tilley sat on that park bench for nearly an hour, his composure slowly returning with each passing minute.

Gonna be ok. Keep my shit together like Mac said. Make my way to a hotel and hunker down there for the night.

Tilley stood up, looking out in front of him again for any signs of trouble. The few people he saw nearby appeared normal. They included another person walking their dog, an older man sitting on another park bench, and a woman walking slowly along a walk path some forty yards from Tilley's location.

Then Tilley spotted Nigel, Dasha Al Marri's personal bodyguard, walking slowly past the man seated on the park bench. Tilley could see Nigel's head moving slowly from right to left, looking for him in the park.

Ray Tilley moved slowly to his left, around the cement wall, making certain to not move too quickly and catch Nigel's attention. Once on the other side, he looked down another red bricked walk path that a sign indicated led to the White House viewing area – the place where protesters were always gathering along Pennsylvania Avenue.

That'll have more people, security, maybe even media.

Tilley glanced behind him and saw no sign of Nigel. Perhaps he had already moved on. The walk path toward the White House viewing area was oddly absent of people though, which caused Tilley to pause momentarily, wondering why the path suddenly felt so isolated. Mere coincidence perhaps - it was nearing the early evening hours after all.

"Let's not have ourselves an unnecessary spectacle Mr. Tilley."

The accent was English, and all too familiar. Nigel stood directly in front of Tilley, his dark eyes glaring back at Tilley with just a hint of disdain.

"Do you understand Mr. Tilley – there is no need for any displays of false bravado now."

Tilley pushed back his fear and stood his ground, staring down the shorter Nigel.

"You keep away from me. Come any closer, and I shoot you dead."

Nigel smiled back, holding his hands out from his sides.

"Oh, I'm certain you would Mr. Tilley, if allowed to do so. Your mistake was talking to others about this you know. We hired you in great part because of your reputation for keeping your mouth shut. You have disappointed us terribly you know. You Americans and your penchant for talk - it'll be the death of you all some day."

Tilley withdrew the handgun from his coat pocket and pointed it at Nigel.

"I'm walking out of this park. Fuck you, and fuck that bitch Dasha."

Nigel's eyes flared angrily as he took a step toward Tilley.

"No need for such language Mr. Tilley. You know nothing of Ms. Al Marri, and are not worthy to speak of her like that. In fact, you are not worthy to speak of her at all."

"Hey! What's going on? You – stay right there!"

Tilley turned to see park security walking toward him. The man appeared young, no more than thirty, dressed in the blue short sleeved dress shirt and slacks common to security personnel of the area. Seeing the security officer offered Tilley a feeling of hope, as it seemed unlikely Nigel would attempt to harm in with such a witness so nearby.

Placing his gun back into his coat pocket, Ray Tilley turned to look back at the park security who now stood no more than ten feet from him.

"This man is threatening me sir. I want him detained and questioned please. I believe he may be armed."

Tilley was shocked to feel Nigel brush past him as he walked toward the security officer. That shock quickly turned to horror as Nigel aimed a gun at the officer and fired, the bullet ripping through the young man's forehead. Tilley's legs were already moving before he thought to do so, running through a batch of trees as the gloom of impending night cast a shadow over the park grounds.

At nearly sixty years of age, Ray Tilley was not accustomed to running so fast, but run he did, even as his heart began to pound painfully in his chest with enough force he feared he may be having a heart attack. He emerged from the trees onto another red bricked walk path, moving as fast as he could, not daring to look behind him. Nigel's gun made almost no sound when it fired, indicating it was silenced, meaning the shot was unlikely to have drawn any attention, and thus, no chance of help.

Your gun doesn't have a silencer though.

Tilley removed his handgun from his pocket and turned to look behind him. There was no sign of Nigel, though the increasing darkness was making it increasingly difficult to see more than forty or so feet in any direction. Tilley raised the gun into the air and fired off two rounds, the sound echoing across the park grounds. Given the park's proximity to the White House, surely the gunfire would alert more security – possibly even Secret Service.

A flash of light erupted from the darkness thirty yards from behind Tilley, followed by the pain of a bullet grazing his upper left arm. He turned to once again run, gasping for breath and waiting for another bullet to rip through his back. Up ahead he saw a well lit area, one of the large statues common to the park grounds. It was of a man atop a horse rearing up onto its hind legs – the Andrew Jackson sculpture. Tilley knew that meant he was nearing the very center of Lafayette Square.

Get to the statue, use the base of it for cover.

The Jackson sculpture was enclosed by a simple, wrought iron fence. The fence's height was nearly as tall as Tilley, the tops of the bars ending in large metallic arrows.

Just need a few seconds to climb over the fence. Just a few seconds…

Ray Tilley glanced behind him again and seeing no sign of being followed, placed his handgun back into his coat pocket and grasped the top of the fence in each hand and began pulling himself up. It took more than a few seconds, but with shaking muscles, and sweat pouring out from him, Tilley felt the grateful thud of his body dropping to the other side of the fence. He was inside the sculpture area, the large granite base of the statue no more than twenty feet away.

Get up and run!

Even though there was no evidence Nigel was nearby, a warning sounded in Tilley's head. It is said all people have a sense of knowing something is there, even if one's eyes tell them otherwise. Ray Tilley's senses were propelling his body forward toward the statue as fast as he legs would carry him.

The first bullet entered the back of his right shoulder, shattering a portion of his collar bone before exiting out from under his armpit. The sensation reminded Tilley of hot candle wax being poured over and then through, his skin.

The second bullet glanced off of his right hip, nicking a bit of bone and burning a small trench across the area. Tilley cried out in pain as he tried to turn his body around to fire back at Nigel, his own handgun now held out in front of him.

The third bullet ripped into Tilley's lower throat, snapping his head back with enough force it propelled his entire body backward, the back of Tilley's head smacking against the granite base of the Andrew Jackson sculpture with enough force to fracture his skull.

One of the last images Ray Tilley could comprehend before death overtook him, were the inscribed words of a plaque imbedded on the side of the sculpture:

OUR FEDERAL UNION
IT MUST BE PRESERVED

Tilley had just enough strength left in his final moments to move his head to the side to be able to view Jackson's visage as it glared back across Lafayette Square and Pennsylvania Avenue, toward the regal and imposing main entrance of the White House. Though he had viewed this sculpture many times as he walked past it over the years, Ray Tilley had never noticed the look of horror that clearly appeared on the former president's face, as if the statue were looking at some terrible monster inhabiting Washington D.C.

Ray Tilley may have not understood that look before, but as the last remnants of his life left his body, he understood then.

XXIV.

Mac Walker sat alongside Ella Lerner inside the confines of the ambassador's black SUV as it made its way swiftly toward the Benina airport. The ambassador intended to return to Tripoli, while Mac and Ella were to meet with the Frenchman Louis Danton, head of the United Nations humanitarian efforts in and around Benghazi, and, if the ambassador's assessment was correct, something of a double agent working to thwart the efforts of the Saudi-funded globalists.

Jack had remained behind with Ella's security team at her office, with instructions to check in with Minnick and Benny back at the safe house on the hour.

Ella sat next to Mac, her face its customary and unreadable portrait. Mac found himself fascinated by what her background story might be. Clearly she was a highly trained agent of the Israelis, and the two men assisting with her security openly showed great respect toward her authority. She knew Tilley somehow, but both she and him were unwilling to provide Mac any details of that knowing.

"No need to stare Mr. Walker."

Mac caught himself doing exactly what Ella accused him of – staring at her face.

"Sorry, I just find you one hell of an interesting woman Ella. Know any quiet bars in Libya where a guy like me and an Israeli woman like you can sit down for a drink and some nice conversation?"

Ella's lips pursed slightly as she struggled to suppress a smile.

Mac eyes wandered to the quickly passing desert landscape outside. He found it odd that an American ambassador would be travelling with so little security to protect him. He only had his driver, a man who appeared no older than thirty and still quite wet behind the ears. Surely the man was a target in a place like Libya, so why the lack of any real security?

The entrance to the Benina Airport, the same one Mac and his men had driven out from just a few days earlier, was less than a half mile ahead. The ambassador turned in his seat to look back at Mac and Ella.

"Mr. Danton is expecting you of course. I've filled him with only the information I believed he needed to know – namely that your team needs access to a flight out of Libya Mac. He has assured me he can provide that within the next twenty four hours, but you'll have to confirm that with him yourself when you meet him."

"And you are certain he can be trusted Mr. Ambassador?"

The ambassador's eyes held Mac's for a moment before he nodded.

"Yes – I give you my word. You have to leave your weapons in the vehicle of course, they'll be there for you when you get back. You can use it to drive yourself back to Ella's office when your finished with your meeting."

The SUV drove past a checkpoint without stopping, indicating airport security had already been informed of the ambassador's arrival. The vehicle pulled into a parking space near a large two story metallic building where two men holding AK-47s stood outside a single white door. Mac's eyes looked up and saw two more armed men looking out from the building's roof top.

After exiting the vehicle, Mac and Ella stood across from the ambassador and his driver. The ambassador pointed a thumb toward the white door entrance to the building.

"Mr. Danton is inside there. I won't be joining you for the meeting – have to catch my flight out of here. Good luck Mr. Walker, and thank you as always Ms. Lerner for you and your government's assistance. Oh – and Mr. Walker…if you find yourself in need of help once you get back to the United States, please call this gentleman. He's an attorney who assists people like yourself. He may be able to help.

Mac looked down at the business card the ambassador has given him, reading the name and phone number.

**Neeson Legal Services
303-237-7788**

The ambassador and his driver were already walking away before Mac could respond. Mac placed the business card in one of his jacket pockets and glanced down at Ella, whose face betrayed a touch of apprehension as she followed the ambassador's departure.

"I hope he is taking adequate precautions. He's been much too confident of himself of late."

Mac, remembering his recent thoughts on the ambassador's lack of security, nodded in agreement at Ella's concerns before the two of them made their way toward the building's entrance. The older of the two armed guards, a tall, thin man in his forties, opened the white door for Mac and Ella, nodding once as they walked past him.

The door opened up to a small, low-ceilinged square room with a set of metallic stairs leading upward. Mac paused at the bottom of the stairs as he looked down at Ella.

"You met this Danton before?"

Ella's eyes were staring upward, trying to determine if anyone could hear them.

"Yes – just once. The ambassador has dealt with him a great deal."

Mac found himself following Ella's gaze upward as well.

"And what was your impression – is he someone you think we can trust?"

Ella's eyes narrowed slightly as she continued to look upward.

"I trust no-one Mr. Walker.

Ella began moving up the stairs, taking them two at a time as Mac followed close behind, failing to prevent himself from looking in appreciation at Ella's well formed and toned backside.

Seconds later and both of them stood outside another white door. A security camera placed in the upper right hand corner stared back at them as they waited. After nearly a minute passed, a voice called out to them from a speaker placed inside the ceiling just above their heads.

"Ms. Lerner and Mr. Walker – please come in!"

The voice's accent was unmistakably French.

The door opened inward a few inches, allowing Ella to push it completely open and her and Mac to step into the adjoining room. Several desks were lined up across the floor, each of them with a man or woman seated and working, the sound of fingers over keyboards filling the space. Narrow windows ran the length of the room, allowing light in as well as providing views of the surrounding airport. From the other side of the space and moving quickly toward them was a tall man similar in age to Mac, with longish black hair lined with more than a bit of grey that was combed back from his prominent forehead. He was dressed in a cream colored suit matched with a brilliant red tie. His feet were home to a pair of equally light grey canvas boat shoes, which he appeared to be wearing without socks.

"Hello! Hello! Hello! I am Louis Danton, master of all you see before you!"

Danton's wide smile revealed brilliant and perfectly aligned white teeth, and his extended right hand was comprised of extremely long and perfectly manicured fingers. Mac caught a wave of cologne as Danton moved toward them, the scent reminding him somewhat of soapy leather.

Louis Danton paused in front of Ella, his eyes looking her up and down as the wide smile remained on his face.

"Oh Ms. Lerner, it has been too long since we saw each other last! You look magnificent! An oasis in this too drab and dangerous place! Please now, the both of you, follow me to my office where we can talk. Would you like food or drink? Coffee?"

Mac noted the faint outline of a gun holster running down the back of Danton's left shoulder. He was armed.

"No thank you Mr. Danton – we don't have much time."

Mac was glad for Ella's refusal of food or drink. He wanted to be out of this place as quickly as possible.

Danton walked briskly back across the room, smiling to some of the workers sitting at their desks as he did so. A dark grey door stood at the other end of the room with a single armed guard standing outside.

"I apologize for the militant look of the place, necessary precaution given the circumstances of course. All my security team are French though – totally trustworthy."

"Yeah – but they start running at the first sign of trouble, right?"

Louis Danton stopped in mid stride, his back straightening. Mac could sense he didn't appreciate the joke. Ella though, offered her widest smile yet, even looking like she might actually laugh.

"I understand one's need to share humor Mr. Walker – but would ask you not do so at your host's expense."

Danton continued making his way toward the door as the armed guard glared back at Mac, indicating he too heard the Mac's joke regarding the French's notorious historical penchant for running away.

Ella and Mac followed Danton into his office, a spacious room that was much more luxuriously furnished than the main second floor area. A large window was placed directly behind Danton's desk, allowing him a full view of the arriving and departing airport traffic.

"Now you two have a seat. Make yourselves more comfortable. If you don't mind, I am going to enjoy a smoke."

The soapy leather smell was more pronounced inside the Danton's office, though it also mingled with that of burning tobacco. Danton stood next to a small drink cart, where he proceeded to fill the glass half full with whiskey.

"You know, most people when they think of France and alcohol, only think of wine, but we produce some of the most marvelous whiskeys. This here is a bottle of single malt from the island of Corsica. Reasonably priced, and frankly, among the best you will find. I've sold thousands of bottles of this very whiskey from this airport alone! By the time I leave here, these Libyans will love it!"

"Thought Muslims didn't drink."

Danton laughed loudly over Mac's comment, followed by a long drink from his glass.

"Muslims? They are like any other religion – you have your hardliners who follow their interpretations of the Koran, and you have everybody else who just wants to get by in this life and enjoy it as much as possible. I'm in the enjoyment business Mr. Walker, among other things."

Mac had figured out Danton's angle.

"You're a smuggler. You use the airport and your United Nations credentials to bring in goods that people need, and in a place like this, all blown to hell, they need a lot. You're getting rich off of the chaos."

Mac could see Ella tense slightly as she glanced at Mac from the corner of her eye.

Danton remained quiet for a moment before breaking out into his wide, brilliant white smile again, waiving his right pointer finger next to his face.

"Yes-yes-yes Mr. Walker! I accept your description, and plead guilty as charged! I assure you though, my interests go far beyond my own profits. I actually do enjoy being able to bring pleasure to others. Providing food, drink, clothing, transportation, computers, or any other assorted gadgetry – is that not what makes this world go round Mr. Walker? I am an unrepentant capitalist you see, both a provider and recipient of the near boundless possibilities of the free market!"

Mac looked back at Danton with a mixture of annoyed amusement. Ella, sensing perhaps that Mac's annoyance might soon overcome that amusement, intervened.

"Mr. Walker and his men seek transport back to the United States Mr. Danton. The ambassador indicated you are both able and willing to provide it."

Louis Danton, who had by then sat down behind his large, oak desk, leaned forward in his chair, his head tilting slightly to the left as he took a closer look at both Mac and Ella.

"You two have a bit of chemistry, don't you? I can see it! Romance in Benghazi – how marvelous! I have long believed there is always time for love. Always!"

Ella had been right – Mac's patience was wearing thin.

"I'm here about getting me and my men out of Libya alive. Let's just focus on that ok?"

Danton took another sip from his glass and then a long, slow drag from his cigarette.

"I can do that Mr. Walker – for a price. This isn't a charity I'm running here you know."

Mac couldn't help but laugh at the irony of Danton's statement.

"You're in charge of the fucking United Nations humanitarian efforts in Benghazi."

Louis Danton leaned still further forward over his desk, both smiling and nodding his head at the same time.

"I know – I know! Such an interesting contradiction don't you think?"

"The ambassador says you're one of us, meaning you are no friend of the globalists that infect the United Nations. That you are working against these radioactive weapons that are here, or heading this way. That true?"

Mac had posed the question for the sole purpose of pushing Danton away from his comfort zone. It didn't work. Danton's mood remained pleasantly aloof, carefree, and completely at ease.

"Yes, that too is true Mr. Walker. I may be a capitalist, but not one without a certain degree of morals and considerations toward the bigger picture. Such weapons should not be part of this program. I am working to circumvent their use, as I have done in the past, and will do so again. As for your description of the United Nations, again, I would agree. It has become a most vile and corrupt institution, and increasingly dangerous to both our countries. Again, I work to alleviate that danger as much as possible, but to do so, I must work within the beast itself Mr. Walker. Does that make sense to you?"

Mac shrugged. He could give a shit about the politics of the United Nations, or supposed conspiracies – he just wanted to get his men home safe from this fucking disaster of an assignment.

"My dad used to tell me you lay down with dogs, you get up with fleas Mr. Danton. Might want to think about that as you spend all this time working within the beast, as you put it."

Louis Danton clapped his hands together and laughed as cigarette smoke swirled around his head.

"Very good Mr. Walker, indeed that too is true! Fleas…yes, there is an abundance of those in this business of mine. Nasty, bloodsuckers they are!"

"And what about Dasha Al Marri – I assume you know about her?"

Finally Danton grew quiet, his eyes losing a touch of their humor.

"Oh yes, Dasha. I know her well Mr. Walker, well enough to know to avoid her if at all possible. A scary one she is. A damn cold piece of work. I understand you recently came to know a bit of her…warmer side though."

Mac's eyes widened in shock. He didn't expect Danton to know about the night and morning he had spent making love to Dasha. Ella's eyes looked over at Mac briefly. Was that disappointment Mac saw looking back at him? Or anger? At least it wasn't indifference."

Danton held up both of his hands in front of him.

"I apologize Mr. Walker, that was not an appropriate comment. Such business is your business, and not mine. Please, forgive me."

"Transport from Benghazi, Mr. Danton. Please confirm when you can provide that."

Ella's request cut through Danton's discomfort, allowing him to change the subject.

"Yes, tomorrow morning. 9:00 a.m. we have a United Nations transport flight leaving here on its way to Abidjan – the Ivory Coast. From there you and your men can access an Air France flight to take you back to the United States. You simply need go to desk two and ask for Gifford Roche. I will already have contacted him for you to let him know your situation and needs. He and I have done a great deal of business together already."

"How much?"

Mac's question was left unanswered as Danton finished the contents of his whiskey glass. His eyes then narrowed slightly as he looked back at Mac.

"Ah, now we enter real negotiations Mr. Walker! Are you up to the challenge?"

Ella stood up, looked down at Mac and then back to Danton.

"No negotiations Mr. Danton. You are doing this as a favor for the ambassador."

For the first time since meeting him, Mac noted a hint of real danger in Danton's voice as he too stood up to stare back at Danton.

"There are always negotiations Ms. Lerner. You asking otherwise will not make it so. As I just said, I am not running a charity here. You wish for me to assist Mr. Walker and his men. That requires some effort, certain risk, for which I expect to me fairly compensated."

Mac placed the envelope of forty thousand Euros given to him at the beginning of the assignment on the top of Danton's desk.

"That's forty thousand Euros. It's all I have."

Louis Danton's hand snatched the envelope and extracted the bills, his fingers expertly counting the amount in just a few seconds.

"Very good Mr. Walker – we now have a deal. I will reserve a spot for you and your men on the flight leaving here tomorrow, September 11th, at 9:00 a.m. Please do not be late Mr. Walker, I will not hold the flight for you. Also be aware that I am not responsible for protecting you between now and then, or at any time during or after the flight. Do you understand?"

Mac nodded.

"Sure, don't get myself killed. I've done a fair job of that so far Mr. Danton, as you have too, apparently."

Danton bowed his head slightly, the warm smile returning.

"That I have Mr. Walker. That I have. If you arrive back here tomorrow by 8:30 I can personally see you and your men onto the flight."

Danton extended his hand to Mac, who shook it firmly in his own. Ella turned abruptly from Danton's desk and began walking toward the door. Once outside they returned to the black SUV left to them by the ambassador. Ella took the wheel, indicating she was more familiar with the Benghazi streets than Mac. He offered no protest, silently taking his place in the passenger seat.

Halfway back to Ella's office, Mac attempted to start a conversation.

"Look, that stuff about Dasha, I didn't think---"

Ella cut Mac off, her voice abrupt, though her face again unreadable.

"Who you choose to sleep with Mr. Walker, however ill advised that choice might be, is no business of mine. I don't care to hear of the details though, so if you don't mind, please drop the subject."

Mac Walker knew, among other things, survival, chaos, weapons, blood, pain, fear, but through all that learning, he would be the first to admit, he didn't know shit about women. They were an ever changing complication that remained a seemingly unending mystery to him.

XXV.

Jack met Mac at the entrance to Ella's office. The look on his face suggested trouble of some sort, making Mac worry over the safety of Minnick and Benny, who had been left at the safe house.

"What it is?"

Jack looked over at Ella and then motioned for Mac to follow him inside. Jack was on edge again, glancing back behind him as Ella closed the entrance door.

"I spoke with Minnick about twenty minutes ago. There has been double the traffic going into that compound. Lots of those big U.N. transport trucks. That's not what's got them spooked though – there were about ten guys walking outside the compound. A few of them were definitely armed, and at least one of them was taking pictures. This went on for about an hour, and then they jumped back into their vehicles and took off. Before they left though, a couple of them walked across the road and were looking right at the safe house and taking more pictures.

It was recon work Mac. A shitty, overly obvious Libyan version of it, but that's what it was. Minnick and Benny think the same. Somebody is planning to move against that compound, and it seems like they suspect they're being watched from the safe house. We need to pull Minnick and Benny the hell out of there like right now. I'll go pick them up myself if I have to."

Mac offered no disagreement. He had already intended to drive out and get Minnick and Benny already.

"We'll both go Jack. Pick them up and bring them back here where we'll wait out the night and then I got us a flight out of here first thing in the morning."

Jack's eyes widened slightly – he appeared hopeful for the first time in a long time.

"Danton check out ok? He can be trusted?"

Mac nodded.

"Yeah – I think so. He's an odd one, but seems to know his way around this shithole well enough. He has a 9:00 set up for the four of us, take us to the Ivory Coast and then we catch an Air France flight back to the States. Figure we leave here tomorrow no later than 8:00 a.m."

Jack offered Mac a genuine smile.

"Best fucking news I've heard since we got here."

Ella walked up to Mac and Jack, her arms folded across her chest.

"So you two will be driving back out to your safe house then?"

Mac nodded.

"Yeah, gonna leave right now. Be back here within the hour, that is, if you don't mind us staying here overnight?"

Ella gave Mac a slight smile and shrugged.

"That will be fine Mr. Walker. You and your men are welcome to stay with us tonight."

After calling Minnick and Benny to let them know they were coming to get them, the drive out to the safe house took less than twenty minutes, due in great part to Jack's penchant for pushing the Hummer to its limit at every opportunity. During one stretch of desert road where the massive SUV neared almost a hundred miles an hour, Jack turned to Mac and grinned widely.

"Drive it like I stole it man!"

Mac laughed, even as his knuckles turned white from his tightening grip on the dashboard.

"You did steal it Alabama."

Soon Jack was driving the Hummer past the gated entrance of the safe house, both he and Mac already holding their handguns at the ready in case of any trouble. Before they reached the entrance steps, both Minnick and Benny were outside, both carrying sniper rifles on their backs, and several boxes of ammunition stuffed into their pockets.

Benny clapped Mac's shoulder as he moved quickly past him toward the Hummer.

"Glad to see you man. Things getting' weird around here Mac. Time to go, time to go!"

Mac's phone began vibrating in his coat pocket. The number indicated it was Stephen Mardian.

"Hello, Mr. Walker. I have further instructions for you."

Mac noted the strain in Mardian's voice. Something was wrong.

"Are you there Mr. Walker?"

"I'm here Mardian – what are the instructions?"

Mardian paused as Mac detected the sound of a brief scuffle coming over the phone. Someone was there with Mardian.

"Mr. Walker, you know the property you have been conducting surveillance on?"

"Yeah."

The strain in Mardian's voice was becoming even more pronounced as he spoke.

"There is a man due to arrive tomorrow afternoon at that location. He is the American ambassador to Libya. We have confirmed he is the one responsible for the weapons transfers in Benghazi. Potentially thousands of weapons Mr. Walker. He has become an extremely dangerous and unpredictable man, who appears to now be working with, and aiding, the anti-American insurgents throughout the region. His actions will cost many lives Mr. Walker, and we are now asking you to reduce that potential number. We need you to save lives Mr. Walker. Do you understand?"

Mac recalled the ambassador telling him he would be receiving a phone call just like the one Mardian was now conducting.

"You're saying you want us to kill a United States ambassador? Are you out of your fucking mind Mardian? We didn't sign up for this shit. No way."

Mac heard more indications of a struggle, and then the unmistakable sound of a gun firing.

"Hello again Mr. Walker."

It was Dasha Al Marri. Mac remained silent.

"Mr. Walker, don't be rude. And don't be one who breaks a deal. We do have a deal Mr. Walker – you took my money, remember?"

Mac could feel his jaw clenching as his hand threatened to squeeze his phone into oblivion.

"Where's Tilley?"

Dasha's voice, with its hint of an English accent, betrayed no fear over Mac's potential fury against her.

"Mr. Tilley became an unreasonable liability to us Mr. Walker. What is it you Americans are so fond of saying – a pain in the ass. So, that liability was remedied. Permanently."

Mac felt gut punched at the news of Tilley's death.

"I'm not doing the assignment Dasha. You and whoever you are working with can go fuck yourselves. And when I get back home, you better not be there, because I'm coming for you, do you understand? You, Nigel, whoever else is behind this – I will kill every one of you myself."

Dasha laughed, the sound making Mac's lip curl into a snarl.

"Oh Mr. Walker – if only your cock were as big as your threats, I might entertain the possibility of keeping you around for entertainment. As it is, I am already entertained enough. You either complete the assignment as agreed, or someone else will and you and your men, will not be allowed to live. Now before you answer, I would suggest you consider my words carefully Mr. Walker, for unlike you, I have the means to see it done. I will kill every one of your men one by one, and allow you to live just long enough to know you were responsible for each of those deaths. So grow up Mr. Walker, and do what you're told. Kill the ambassador, and save your men."

Mac ended the call, the adrenalin coursing through his body, making it difficult for him to think clearly. Benny, sensing how enraged the call had made Mac, was the first to question who it was.

"Something wrong with Tilley, Mac?"

Mac took a slow deep breath and looked back at Benny as he nodded his head slowly.

"Yeah – he's dead. Pretty sure Dasha had him killed. Think Mardian's dead too."

Minnick's face expressed confusion.

"Wait – I just heard you talking to Mardian. How can he be dead?"

Mac closed his eyes briefly, still working on calming himself down to ensure he was thinking clearly.

"I was. Heard a gunshot, and then he wasn't talking no more. It was Dasha."

Mac shared the details of Dasha's threats, as well as the information he had acquired from both the ambassador and Louis Danton. When he finished, Benny, Jack, and Minnick stood silently staring back at Mac. Benny looked particularly shocked at what Mac told him.

"My god Mac, if these people think they can kill someone like Stephen Mardian…I mean c'mon man, that guy is connected! Right? Talking about a man who hangs with Senators, who gets invited to dinners at the fucking White House. This woman, this Dasha Al Marri, she's got enough power to kill off someone like Mardian? How the hell is something like that…"

Benny's words trailed off as he continued to stare at Mac, looking for some semblance of sanity in their world gone mad. Jack's voice ripped through the silence left by Benny, his tone both angry and fearful.

"I told you! Told you this was all wrong. We don't do work for the fucking United Nations, or some Middle East bitch! This government is all fucked up. Been that way for years now. We all knew it, but we didn't want to admit it, right? We were getting paid good, living large, all that shit. Well now what? They ain't gonna let us just waltz on out of here. Not with what we know. They're coming for us, and it's gonna be soon. Fucking Benghazi Mac! I told you dammit!"

Despite Jack's understandable concern, Mac found himself more relaxed than he had been just moments before. He looked back at his men and offered a small, knowing smile, his eyes crackling with the energy of a man ready, and more important, willing, to go into battle.

"Let them threaten us. Fact is, we just might be the four baddest motherfuckers walking this earth today, am I right? They want to come after us Jack? Fine, let them get a taste of what we do. Let them know the hell we can bring."

XVI.

The hours waiting in Ella's building passed slowly. Though Mac and his men attempted to rest in shifts, none of them were able to fall asleep. They all sensed something would be coming their way. As Jack had said earlier, there was simply no chance they would be allowed to just waltz out of Benghazi knowing what they did. Mac didn't fear a fight, though he did fear putting Ella and her men in greater danger than they already faced on a day to day basis.

"We can leave here Ella – you don't have to let us stay. I've put you in a tough position here and I don't want you to get hurt because of it."

Ella sat on a small cot that she used for a bed in one of the smaller rooms of the building. The room had no windows, just a door, the cot, and a single lamp. She raised her face upward slightly as she sat on the cot looking back at Mac.

"You think your purpose here and mine are so different Mr. Walker? We have been tracing the transport of weapons for some time, and like your Mr. Tilley, and Louis Danton, find the access to radioactive devices something we cannot simply allow to go unchecked. My life and those of my men have been in increasing danger since we arrived here. It is what I do Mr. Walker – much the same as what you do. Though I am happy to know, that I am afforded the protection of my own government, while you and your men appear to be endangered by yours."

Mac found himself nodding in agreement to Ella's words. Yes, the American government was in a complete shambles these days. An incoherent mess of a foreign policy that was putting everyone in danger, from citizens to soldiers, they were all suffering under years of anti-Americanism both at home and abroad.

"If you get out of Libya Mr. Walker, what then?"

Mac had been considering that very question for the last several hours. What then indeed. With both Tilley and Mardian likely gone, Mac and his team had few contacts within the government to turn to, certainly none who they could trust.

"Not sure – we'll have to lay low. Watch our back, and see what happens."

Ella's face lost its unreadable mask, allowing Mac to sense her sadness at the future that awaited him.

"Not much of a life Mr. Walker, always wondering if and when someone comes for you. It will be as if you are still on an assignment, though the enemy is your own government."

Mac leaned against the wall opposite Ella's cot and took a deep breath.

"Yeah, though I know we won't be the first people dealing with that scenario. Maybe things will change. A new election, a new way of looking at the world. Who knows…"

Ella shook her head slowly.

"Perhaps, but unlikely. Tell me Mr. Walker, what do you really want once you get back to America?"

Mac's answer came to him more quickly than he anticipated.

"To be left the hell alone. I want a place I can go and just…relax. Just be myself, do what I want, and for the government to let me be. That's it. I've seen all I want to see of this world. Done things I don't want to think about. A little peace and quiet is all I want now, a little time to strum my guitar, a strong cup of coffee, a good burger, some cold beer. Man…that sounds like paradise to me right now."

Ella smiled, her eyes illuminated by a warmth Mac had known was hidden inside her cold exterior.

"You want what the world once saw in America Mr. Walker. Opportunity, freedom, and the space to be left alone. Perhaps if you find that place again, you can invite me to visit you."

Mac held Ella's gaze and smiled back.

"I'd like that Ella. I'd like that a lot."

Gunfire sounded from above them.

Ella jumped from her cot as Mac, with his handgun drawn, opened the door and stepped into the hallway. Udi was already running toward them holding an assault rifle.

"We've spotted at least ten men setting up a perimeter outside – all armed."

Ella's icy exterior had returned. She was all business, her training taking over.

Mac looked at his watch, noting it was just past four in the morning.

"I want to check it out Ella. See what they're doing out there."

Ella nodded to Mac, and then disappeared down the hall. Mac ran in the opposite direction, bounding up the narrow stairs of the roof access. Once on the roof, he crouched low, making his way slowly to the roof's edge facing the street below. The second member of Ella's security team was already there on his stomach, his assault rifle held out in front of him. Mac crept alongside the Israeli's right side, peering out from the rooftop.

As Udi had indicated downstairs, there were at least ten armed men just across the street, spread out some twenty yards apart from one another. This was no Libyan mob – the men below had some training, though the darkness made it difficult to determine their skin color.

The Israeli man next to Mac extended his right hand to him.

"Hello, my name is Tamir. I don't think we've been introduced yet."

Mac shook the man's hand firmly, realizing he hadn't known the Israeli's name until now. Tamir appeared to be around thirty years of age, similar in height and build to Mac, with , with a clean shaven face and dark, closely cropped hair. A long thin scar ran along his left cheek almost down to his jaw.

"Well Tamir, who do you think those men are down there?"

Tamir grunted.

"Saudis."

Mac continued to peer down at the deliberate movement of the men below.

"Saudis? How do you know that?"

The tone of Tamir's response indicated his certainty.

"Heard them speaking. Definitely Saudis. See the outline of their weapons? M16A1 – standard issue for Saudi Special Forces. Those men down there are not active Saudi military though. They are like you, contract soldiers, likely sent here from the Saudi embassy in Tripoli."

"So what's your plan Tamir?"

Tamir smiled and shrugged.

"That's up to them. They fire on us, we fire back. Otherwise, we simply wait and see."

Mac looked at his watch again.

"I've got a plane to catch in about four hours."

Both Mac and Tamir turned to look behind them as Udi was making his way toward them with the MG-42 machine gun Ella had used from this same rooftop position to scatter the Libyan mob days ago.

Udi set the weapon up to the right of Tamir, pausing to scan the area below them as well. He glanced over at Tamir and then nodded his head in the direction of the Saudis.

"Anything different?"

Tamir shook his head.

"No – same thing. They have a perimeter set up, but nothing more. No sign yet they intend to attack."

Udi placed his hand on Tamir's shoulder and squeezed it firmly.

"If they do, Ella wants you to blow them to hell."

Mac decided to follow Udi back to the building's main level, certain his men would want an update. Jack was the first one to meet him in the hallway, one of the sniper rifles held in his right hand.

"What do we got Mac?"

Mac tipped his head in the direction of the reception area so he could address Jack, Benny, and Minnick at the same time. Benny and Minnick were both standing on either side of the entrance door. When they saw Mac, they walked over to him and stood next to Jack.

"There's about ten men outside. They appear to be armed with M16s. Tamir, the other member of Ella's crew, thinks they are hired Saudi guns. So far, they aren't making any move – just seem to be waiting us out."

Jack jabbed his left thumb in the air in the direction of the door.

"We ain't missing that flight out of here Mac. I'll shoot them dead myself before I let that happen."

Mac nodded back at Jack.

"I feel the same way Jack. Don't worry, if it comes to that, that's what we'll do. Udi already has the MG-42 set up on the roof."

Minnick's eyes narrowed as he glanced upward.

"Those men outside have to already know about the machine gun Mac. If all they have are some M16s, no way they have the firepower to take us out. The Israeli's could rip apart half the street with that thing."

Mac considered Minnick's words. He was right – the Saudis either had no intention of going at them in a firefight – or they had some other plan. Not knowing what that plan could be made Mac increasingly uneasy.

"I need to speak with Ella. Anything we do, impacts her and her men. We owe her the opportunity to be a part of that discussion."

Benny nodded his head.

"Agreed. She's helped to keep our ass alive."

Jack and Minnick glanced at Benny and then also nodded in agreement.

Mac made his way back down the hallway toward Ella's room. The door was closed, though he could hear her voice from inside the room. Mac knocked lightly.

"Ella, it's Mac. I wanted to discuss possible options."

The door opened, revealing Ella talking into a cell phone. She motioned with her right hand for Mac to come in.

"Understood. The Bulgarian Consulate. Thank you. Yes, I understand. They already have a flight out this morning. Thank you sir."

Ella ended her call and sat down again on the room's cot, as she waited for Mac to speak.

"Who was that?"

"That, Mr. Walker, was my superior. I have instructions to relocate myself and my men to the Bulgarian consulate. We have allies there who will provide my team further security."

Mac considered Ella's words. She intended to stay in Benghazi – but his team was to get the hell out.

"Your team – but not mine, right?"

Ella nodded.

"Correct. We are not to bring you to the Bulgarian consulate Mr. Walker. They don't want the diplomatic dilemma such a visit could create."

There was a light knock on Ella's door. When it opened, Udi stepped inside the small room.

"Ella, the men outside are pulling back. No reason as to why, but they appear to be moving back their positions another hundred yards away from us."

Ella looked at Mac.

"Any ideas?"

Mac was already moving toward the door.

"Don't know, but I want to go take a look."

Udi followed behind Mac as both men made their way quickly back to the rooftop where they found Tamir and Minnick laying on their stomachs peering down into the street below.

Mac crawled alongside Minnick.

"Udi says they are pulling back. Any idea why?"

Minnick was using the night vision scope on his sniper rifle to scan the area.

"No. Guy pulled up in a black SUV a few minutes ago. Got out, was talking into a phone, and then started motioning for everyone to pull back."

Mac could see men moving across a side street nearly eighty yards from Ella's building. He saw no sign of the black SUV Minnick had just described.

"Was he American?"

Minnick nodded.

"Pretty sure – yeah. Didn't get a real good look at him, he was standing behind the SUV most the time. He acted like he was in charge though, no doubt about that."

Without having to ask for further information, Mac knew the man Minnick had spotted was Densmore. Mr. FBI was out in front of a CIA operation and barking orders to a bunch of well armed and well trained Saudis in the streets of Benghazi in front of a building being run by Israeli Special Intelligence.

This is one hell of a mess you got yourself into Mac Walker.

Udi had been looking out into the streets with his own pair of binoculars. His mouth was curled slightly downward as he looked from left to right, and then back again.

"I did reconnaissance work just outside Rafah, right before the ground invasion. My team got caught too far ahead of the line. We were holed up in this abandoned two story home for almost three days, trading rounds with a group of militants whose numbers were growing by the hour. They had us pinned down, but were too afraid of just coming at us directly. Then they backed off. Just like that, after three days of shooting at us, they disappeared. My commanding officer, who was old enough to have served in the South Lebanon Conflict in the early 1990's, ordered us to evacuate the house and run like hell."

Minnick removed his eye from the night vision scope to glance over at Udi.

"And what happened?"

Udi continued to stare into the street below them as he answered.

"We did as we were ordered to do – we ran like hell. They fired at us over and over again, and we simply ran and fired back. Lost two of our team, a few more injured. But we made it past them, knew we were no more than a half mile from Israeli forces. Knew the militants wouldn't follow us. I was looking back from where we had come from, and saw the explosion. Felt it below my feet too. Military forensics tested the site a week later after the area was secured. The building we had been holed up in, was nearly gone. The detonation device was an enhanced Fajr-5 missile, one of the first to be used in the conflict – Iranian made, terrorist enhanced."

While Minnick appeared uncertain as to the intent of Udi's story, the realization hit Mac, turning his blood cold. His head lifted toward the dark Benghazi sky.

"Oh shit."

XVII.

Mac Walker didn't so much run down the stairs as he did fly down them. They needed to get the hell out of the building – and fast.

"Ella! Lock and load time! Does this place have a back way out of here?"

Ella seemed to know that whatever had Mac so spooked was not to be questioned. Perhaps her own instincts had already been telling her something was wrong with how the men had retreated outside.

"Yes – in the bathroom. Under the rug."

Mac was already moving again, his body a blur moving at incredible speed down the hallway. He opened the bathroom door and threw back the rug to reveal the faint outline of panel cut with great precision through the poured concrete flouring. A single brass handle was located in the center of the panel. Mac grasped the handle and pulled upward with a grunt as he removed the solid concrete panel from the floor, exposing a narrow square opening just wide enough to allow a man access through it.

Mac placed two fingers to his mouth and whistled loudly.

"Let's go! Move your asses! Bring weapons and ammo with you!"

Jack was the first to arrive in the bathroom. Mac stepped aside and motioned toward the opening.

"Get down there and wait. We're all right behind you Alabama."

Jack struggled momentarily to fit through the escape route, but then dropped down into darkness as Ella pushed both Udi and Tamir into the hole right behind Jack. Minnick and Benny were the next to drop down into the opening after Mac screamed for them to get moving. That left Mac and Ella looking at one another.

"Your turn Ella."

Ella Lerner stared back at Mac, the faintest of a smile appearing on her face. What she did next shocked Mac Walker, and he was not one to shock easily.

Ella grasped both sides of Mac's face in her hands and brought her lips forcefully against his own. Before she pulled away from the fierce kiss, she bit down on Mac's lower lip with enough force to draw a bit of blood.

"Just in case one or both of dies tonight Mr. Walker."

Mac found himself grinning stupidly at the space where Ella once was as she disappeared into the passage below. Recovering from Ella's kiss, Mac slid his body into the opening.

The escape route was a narrow tunnel that was part of a long abandoned storm drain system. It was no more than three feet in height, requiring Mac and the others to crouch low as they made their way slowly toward what appeared to be a shaft of murky light some fifty yards ahead. As they neared the light, Mac could see it was coming from a metallic grate, a grate Udi was already pushing out from its frame.

One by one, each member of the group pulled themselves through the grate's opening and emerged in a trench that ran alongside the same street that crossed in front of Ella's building. Minnick was already looking out from the trench with his night scope to see if anyone had noticed their escape. After a few seconds, he slid his body fully back down into the trench, then whispered to the others what he saw.

"No sign of anyone. The Hummer is right across from our position here."

Mac nodded back to Minnick and motioned for everyone to follow him to the Hummer.

Pulling himself out of the trench, Mac confirmed what Minnick had just reported. The street appeared empty. That good fortune did nothing to make Mac feel any better. It only confirmed to him that they were running out of time.

With Mac in the lead, the group made their way as quickly yet quietly as possible across the street. The light of the approaching morning was beginning to remove from them the still much needed cover of darkness.

Benny was the first to pause in the street, just steps from the Hummer, his head tilted slightly to the right.

"You hear that?"

Without thinking, Mac was holding his breath as he strained to hear what Benny was talking about. Soon he too made out a faint buzzing noise coming from an unknown location above them as Minnick scanned the early dawn sky with his sniper rifle scope.

"Three hundred yards southeast and approaching. Drone – predator class. It's armed."

Mac pointed to the other side of the Hummer.

"Over here. Get as low as you can behind the vehicle and don't move."

The sound of the drone increased considerably as it approached their location from above, its sound similar to that of a large, angry mosquito. Mac and the others watched as a single missile shot from below the drone's right wing flew into the front of Ella's building.

The explosion was massive, sending fragments of the building flying into the air and then falling down where Ella, Mac, and their men were crouched behind the SUV. The heat from the detonation ripped through the air around them, blowing out the Hummer's windows and causing the vehicle to momentarily rock back and forth on its wheels.

Ella's eyes glared back at the departing drone, her jaw flexing in rage.

"That's your fucking government Mr. Walker. The same one that had my country's Prime Minister enter the White House through the back door."

Mac simply shrugged.

"That's about right. Now let's get the hell out of here. Jack, see if this thing will still fire up."

Jack moved into the driver's seat and turned the ignition, his face breaking out into a mad grin when the big American-made, Vortec V8 rumbled to life.

"Told you Mac! Knew it was a good idea to snag these wheels!"

Mac watched the street as the others positioned themselves inside the SUV before finally taking his place in the passenger seat in the front with Jack.

"Countin' on you to get us the hell outta here Alabama."

Jack slammed the Hummer into gear and slammed his foot down onto the accelerator.

"Like I stole it Mac! Like I fucking stole it!"

As the Hummer leapt forward onto the street, Mac heard multiple gunshots from behind them followed by the sound of bullets ripping into the Hummer's tailgate and rear bumper.

"Heads down!"

The others followed Mac's command immediately, as Jack turned the vehicle sharply to the right, driving across a median and onto another street as the V8 engine roared under the strain of Jack's demands. Mac looked into the passenger rear view mirror and saw two more of the now familiar government issued black SUVs attempting to follow them.

None inside of the Hummer said anything as Jack maneuvered them around parked cars, across lawns, and even down and back up several large irrigation ditches as he worked his way toward the main road leading to Benina Airport. Once onto that main road, Mac looked back again and saw no vehicles behind them.

They passed a sign indicating the airport was eight kilometers away. Jack smiled again as he slapped his hand down hard onto the dashboard as the speedometer indicated they were travelling at nearly eighty miles an hour.

"Just a few more minutes and we're there Mac, and on our way out of this shithole!"

Having done extensive work throughout both Iraq and Afghanistan in recent years, Mac Walker was all too familiar with the effects of an IED. Easy to make, easy to hide, and easy to have detonated when travelled over, they became by far the number one killer of American soldiers in those two wars.

The Hummer's left front tire was lifted entirely off of the road surface as the explosion twisted the metal framing of the driver area inside the vehicle's cabin. Both doors on the left side blew inward several inches, sending bits of metal from one end of the cabin to the other. The SUV's entire frame groaned as the left tire blew out, slamming the left front axle onto the paved surface of the road, sending sparks shooting up as the Hummer's momentum continued forward.

Mac watched as Jack, his head and face already bleeding from several chunks of metal that were imbedded into his flesh and skull, fought to keep the vehicle from turning over onto its side. His face grimaced with the effort as his lips pulled back from his teeth in a bloody snarl.

Finally the Hummer came to a stop on the right side of the road, the steel frame of the front left corner ripped apart by the roadside bomb. Mac pushed the passenger door open as his right hand held his handgun, yelling for everyone to get out. It took no more than a few seconds for everyone to exit the SUV and take cover behind it.

Everyone that is, except for Jack.

Mac made his way back to the open passenger door and peered inside.

"Jack! You need to get out of there!"

Jack Thompson looked back at his friend and team leader Mac Walker and shook his head as he moved his right arm to reveal the large piece of metal that was jammed deeply into the left side of his abdomen. When he spoke, Mac instantly recognized the sound. It was the voice of a human being quickly nearing death, and fully aware of its arrival.

"Not gonna happen Mac."

Benny and Minnick stood beside Mac, looking in at Jack's wound.

"Oh shit no. Goddammit no!"

Benny turned away, both of his hands covering his eyes. Minnick stood silently, though his lower lip trembled slightly as his hands clenched tightly at his sides.

There were no profound words to be uttered by Jack Thompson when death arrived. He was simply there, and then, he wasn't. Mac watched as Jack's eyes fluttered briefly, and then remained open and unblinking. His hands fell from his lap and remained on the driver's seat, while his body slumped forward, a slight wheezing sound escaping his mouth as the last bit of air from his lungs was released.

"We have company Mr. Walker."

It was Ella who now stood next to Mac, her hand on his shoulder.

"The ones who did this, the ones who killed Jack, are now coming to finish the job."

Mac's eyes looked down the road at the two approaching black SUV's, certain one of them contained Mark Densmore. It was Densmore who was in charge of whatever shit was going on in Benghazi. Densmore who had the pull to order a drone strike against Ella's building, and Densmore who set up the explosive device that killed Jack.

Mac Walker grabbed one of the sniper rifles from the back of the Hummer and began walking slowly down the middle of the road toward the quickly approaching SUVs.

It was killing time…

XVIII.

The first shot from the sniper rifle found its mark as the fifty caliber round plunged through the front windshield of the black SUV to Mac's right, ripping through the left side of the driver's skull and then blowing out the rear left passenger window as it exited the interior cabin. The initial kill shot set off a chain reaction where the SUV on the right careened sharply into the other SUV, the dead body of its driver slumped forward against the steering wheel.

The second SUV swerved to avoid being hit, nearly losing control completely and running into the ditch that ran alongside the road. Mac calmly aimed the sniper rifle and fired again.

The second shot missed its mark as the bullet tore off a chunk of the SUV's roof, sending a spray of sparks and metallic fragments into the air. Mac took a deep breath, held it, and fired for a third time.

The bullet split the middle of the windshield, blew a fist sized hole in the chest of one of the men seated in the back, before imbedding itself in the rear tailgate. Mac knew the speed of the SUV left him with just one more shot before the vehicle would be right on top of him.

The fourth shot was aimed at the passenger. Mac was able to look through the sniper rifle's scope and see Densmore looking panicked as he screamed at the driver to run Mac over. The image brought a small smile to Mac's face as he prepared to pull the trigger again.

A bullet skimmed Mac's right arm. The shot had come from one of the men from the first SUV Mac had fired at. The vehicle sat motionless on the side of the road some fifty yards away as three men emerged from it with guns, looking for a fight, all three pointing their weapons directly at Mac as the other SUV was now just twenty feet away and closing very fast.

Mac Walker had no choice but to jump and roll to his left to both avoid being shot and or driven over. He chose the left side knowing the passing SUV would then provide him a brief second of cover from the three armed men moving toward him. As he shifted back onto his left knee, already aiming the rifle for another shot, he spotted Minnick making his way down the ditch, attempting to get behind the three armed men. At the same time Mac heard Benny, Ella, and her men firing several rounds into the passing SUV.

Mac's next shot blew half the head off of one of Densmore's men, while Minnick just as quickly ended the lives of the other two. That left Densmore and whoever else remained alive in the second SUV.

Mac pushed himself back onto his feet and made his way quickly to where Ella and the others stood pointing their weapons at Densmore's vehicle that sat unmoving in the middle of the road nearly a hundred yards from their position. Mac could hear its motor was still running, but detected no movement from inside.

Ella turned to Mac, her own assault rifle resting against her right shoulder.

"Suggestions on how you wish to proceed Mr. Walker?"

Mac used his rifle scope to look over the motionless SUV. Its darkened windows still made it difficult to determine how many, if any, were still alive inside. Udi stood next to Mac also looking at the vehicle through a pair of binoculars.

"Front right tire is blown. Nothing left but the rim."

Udi was right, the SUV's tire had blown apart.

Mac reloaded his rifle and began walking toward the vehicle.

"Spread out, ten yards apart, all weapons at the ready. Anything moves inside there, kill it. Otherwise, wait on my order."

Mac walked slowly toward the SUV as the others in the group followed alongside him. He felt a stinging pain in his right bicep and realized he had forgotten about the bullet that had skimmed him moments earlier. He looked down and scowled at the wound.

Stop bleeding you little bitch.

The back window of the SUV blew out as several rounds of gunfire were shot from inside of it. Mac, Ella, and the others crouched low to the ground and brought their own weapons up and returned fire. Multiple bullet holes ripped through the black SUVs metallic skin as more of its windows shattered into fragments.

Mac held up his left hand to halt the gunfire. Again there was no movement from inside the SUV until after nearly two minutes, the passenger door opened and a man crawled out.

It was Mark Densmore.

Densmore stood up slowly, his right arm braced against the door frame of the vehicle.

"You shouldn't be here Walker!"

Mac began walking slowly toward Densmore while keeping an eye out for any threats from inside the SUV.

"I was thinking the same thing about you Densmore. What the hell is FBI doing running around Benghazi? You here to solve crimes, or committing them?"

Densmore moved away from the black SUV, his steps somewhat unsteady as he wiped away a layer of blood from his upper forehead.

"Look Walker, you can't kill me. I've already called this in. They know all about you and your team. They know about THIS right now. You understand? You kill me and they have you for murdering a federal agent. You and your team, you all go down. You got no protection back home. Tilley's gone. Mardian too. They might let you go, you're just a small bug in all of this, but you kill me – that can't be allowed to just happen Walker. So be a smart guy for once, and just let me walk out of here. Do yourself a favor, do your team a favor, and we all just walk away from this."

Mac stood no more than forty feet from Densmore.

"Can't do that Densmore. You killed one of my men. That don't sit right with me, you know? See, in my world, we don't cut deals with little fucking shits like you. No, we do the world a favor and kill them. Kill them fucking dead."

Densmore glared back at Mac, his face twisted in contempt.

"You're so stupid Walker. So fucking dumb. What's going on out here, it's so much bigger than you could ever imagine. Do you know the powers involved in this? Do you know what will happen to you? You kill me, it won't make a bit of difference. There's a new world coming Walker, and you're either living in it or dead. It's gonna happen. It IS happening. Killing me won't change that. It'll just make it worse for you and anyone or anything you care about."

Mac lowered his rifle, looking Densmore up and down slowly as he shook his head.

"There ain't a bit of man left in you Densmore. Look at you, begging for mercy, making threats that some higher ups are gonna come and get me and my men. Is it worth it to you? Working for this kind of government that would kill its own so easily? You think they won't let me live? What about you? It's just sad seeing you like this – you got no fucking soul left, man. Whatever you were all those years ago, it's gone. Dead. You been dead for years but just didn't know it. Sold out. Maybe there's nothing left for me anymore in America. You could be right about that, but I aim to find out one way or the other. As for you…"

Mark Densmore finally made his move. Mac had intentionally lowered his rifle, knowing Densmore was hiding a handgun tucked into the back of his pants. Even a shit like Densmore deserved a fighting chance – Mac's code of honor required he give him that.

Not that Densmore had any real hope of outdrawing Mac Walker. The former Navy SEAL rested the sniper rifle barrel in his left hand, which allowed his right hand the freedom to pull out his own handgun at a speed too fast for Densmore's eyes to follow. Densmore froze with his own weapon raised up halfway between the ground and Mac, his eyes wide in terror at knowing his life was soon to end.

"No-no-no-no Walker! Don't do it! I can get you out of here! Protect you! All of you! You kill me, they'll come for you! All of you!"

Mac, the death of Jack still front and center in his mind, gritted his teeth as he glowered back at Densmore.

"Shut up."

The bullet entered Densmore's still speaking mouth, exiting the lower base of his skull in a spray of blood and bone. For a half second, Mark Densmore seemed stunned Mac had actually pulled the trigger, his mouth opening and closing wordlessly as he attempted to speak yet again. Then his body crumpled to the paved road below his feet where it remained motionless.

Benny, Minnick, Ella and her men were already making certain no other men were alive inside the second SUV. Two bodies were found and pulled out, both killed by gunshot wounds. They did the same with the other black SUV, pulling three more dead bodies out onto the pavement.

Minnick looked over each one closely, checking to see the weapons issued, their clothing, and cell phones.

"These are all U.S. government Mac. Every one."

Mac didn't bother to look down at the bodies.

"Yeah – figured they would be. Get Jack out of the Hummer and into whichever one of these other vehicles that can still drive. We got a plane to catch."

Mac, Benny, Minnick, Ella, Udi and Tamir sat inside of the first SUV Mac had shot at that day, with Jack's body lying in the back as they drove into the Benina Airport facility. They were stopped by several armed United Nations security guards at the gate. Mac leaned his head out the window and growled to the guard who appeared to be in charge.

"We're here to see Mr. Danton. He's expecting us."

The armed men were looking over the many bullet holes that riddled the SUV's exterior like a series of steel framed pock marks. Mac overheard a familiar, French-accented voice coming from one of the guard's communication devices.

"Let them in!"

No sooner had Mac brought the vehicle to a stop next to the entrance to Louis Danton's office did Danton himself emerge from the second story stairs and make his way down to greet Mac and the others, a genuine look of relief on his face.

"I wasn't certain I would be seeing you this morning Mr. Walker. I had been told your arrival here was not to be allowed by others. It appears you didn't listen. Am I to assume Mr. Densmore is no longer among the living, and that he perhaps met his demise on the road to Benina?"

Mac nodded.

Danton's perfectly aligned and brilliant white teeth revealed themselves in a wide smile as he nodded back at Mac.

"Very good then Mr. Walker! You know, it is a sad but undeniable fact that militant bandits have become quite common in these parts. I will be sure to file a report of the tragic loss of Mr. Densmore and his men to such bandits."

Mac smiled faintly but then nodded toward the SUV.

"I lost a man today Mr. Danton. I need a couple of favors from you if you don't mind."

Louis Danton stood in front of Mac and held his gaze as he replied.

"Whatever you need Mr. Walker. I believe whatever help I might provide you at this moment will be the last help you receive from anyone for some time. The United States is not the country you once knew it to be, but I assure you, I will have you returned there safely.

Mac Walker closed his eyes at Danton's remark about America, knowing all too well how true his words were. Mac felt himself returning to a home no longer his own.

XXIX.

Mac, Benny, and Minnick sat in the back cargo area of the Air France flight Danton had coordinated to take them from the Ivory Coast to the United States. On the floor of the plane lay a simple pine casket where Jack's body was stored.

Before boarding the flight from Benghazi to the Ivory Coast, Mac had taken a moment to thank both Udi and Tamir, and then say goodbye to Ella. She and her men were to be driven to the Bulgarian consulate in Benghazi for protection.

"Stay alive Mac Walker. This world needs more men like you."

Mac looked back at Ella and grinned.

"I think a few more like you would do us all a lot more good Ella. Thank you for your help - for everything."

The two didn't kiss, or embrace. They simply looked at one another for a few more brief moments, and then walked away.

Hours later, as Mac sat with his remaining team around Jack's casket, he poured each of them a shot glass of Jack Daniels whiskey, provided to them as one of the two favors Mac had asked of Louis Danton. The second favor was soon to begin as the song *Sweet Home Alabama* began to blare from the speakers hung in the cargo area of the plane.

Mac raised his glass and watched as Benny and Minnick did the same.

"To Jack Thompson, a big corn fed son-of-a-bitch who I'm gonna miss like hell."

Mac was surprised to feel tears stinging the corners of his eyes as he struggled to continue with the toast.

"Jack didn't want this mission, but he came anyways, for no other reason than I asked him to. I've got to live with that fact for the rest of my life. None us know how long that might be. We're heading back to a country that seems intent on selling itself out to the highest bidder. But, we'll make sure to get Jack back to his people, where he can be laid to rest right. He would of done the same for any of us. That's what soldiers do. We're brothers. We finish the mission. Goddammit, I'm so sorry Alabama. So sorry…"

Mac drank the whiskey and then poured another, and then another.

It was late morning of September 12th when Mac sat around a table inside of an airport bar just an hour after arriving back in the United States. Louis Danton had made good on his promise to deliver them home safely.

Mac's phone rang. It was Ella.

"Mr. Walker, are you in the United States?"

Mac sensed the strain in Ella's voice.

'Yeah – what's the matter?"

"Have you seen the news yet?"

Mac glanced up at Benny and Minnick who sat silently looking back at him.

"Can one of you turn on the news?"

Benny rose from his seat and asked one of the bar staff to turn on a news channel. Mac looked at the images of a burning building on the screen. He knew it instantly. He and his men had sat directly across the road inside of a safe house watching trucks drive into and out of the very same Benghazi compound the news report was showing footage of having been attacked.

The familiar face flashed across the screen. Mac instantly recognized the man, having just spoken to him little more than twenty four hours earlier. The ambassador was dead. The newswoman indicated the administration was placing blame for the attack some unknown Internet video.

"Are you seeing the news reports Mac?"

Mac watched three more faces scroll across the TV – three more dead Americans.

"They're blaming a video."

Ella's laughter held no humor. She sounded incredibly tired.

"Yes, they are. It was a coordinated attack Mr. Walker. I've already seen the intelligence report. A representative from the Turkish government met the ambassador one hour before he died. He was trying to halt the operation and they killed him. There was all kinds of communications chatter. A stand down order. Three others who knew of the operation were killed as well. All Americans. And the explosions, it wasn't mortar fire. It was drones. We have two witnesses who already indicated they spotted a low flying armed drone heading for the second building – the CIA annex. It was drone bombed. Your government attacked and killed its own operatives. The weapons have already been cleaned out. All of them."

Mac could feel his pulse slamming against his temple.

"Are the Israeli's going to come forward with this Ella?"

Ella paused, and then whispered a single word.

"No."

Mac knew that was to be her response before he asked the question.

"They're walking away from this?"

"Yes Mr. Walker. I'm being removed from Benghazi within the hour. There will be no report. Nothing. They want nothing to do with this. It's all been…it's all been a waste. Everything we did, tried to do…nothing."

Mac remained silent, still watching the images of the burning Benghazi compound.

"They'll come for you Mr. Walker. You - your team."

Mac nodded to himself.

"I know."

"What will you do Mac?"

Mac took a deep breath, exhaled slowly, and closed his eyes.

"Do what I've always done Ella.

Stay alive…"

End.

NOW AVAILABLE from D.W. ULSTERMAN:

MAC WALKER'S BETRAYAL:
(Sequel to Mac Walker's Benghazi)

HE SERVED, SACRIFICED, AND BLED FOR HIS GOVERNMENT.
NOW THAT GOVERNMENT WANTS HIM DEAD.

OTHER BOOKS BY D.W. ULSTERMAN:

-DOMINATUS

-TUMULTUS

-THE SECOND OLDEST PROFESSION
LUST. POWER. POLITICS.

http://dwulsterman.com

FREE EXCERPT

THE SECOND OLDEST PROFESSION
The Collection

Lust. Power. Politics.

Noted bestselling political writer D.W. Ulsterman takes readers into the torrid underbelly of Washington D.C., where powerful figures exist in a world dominated by power and lust, and winning is the only rule that matters.

Colin O'Shea is the young, politically talented new addition to a longtime congressman's D.C. staff. He soon finds himself immersed in dealings of deception and intrigue at the highest levels of national politics, and a too - willing participant in the life of a beautiful and dangerous prostitute.

"This story was hot!!! It's like 50 Shades had a one night stand with C-Span!"
-PC

Adult Content

…Cocaine is a hell of a drug. Frank Bennington knew well the feeling of waking up to a head and body aching after a night spent snorting line after line of his longtime medicinal friend. He was an addict – had been for most of his adult life.

Yeah, well who gives a shit? I'm Frank fucking Bennington asshole - politico extraordinaire.

Frank forced his sixty three year old and forty pounds overweight body up from the mattress of his king sized bed, his head blaring out its unhappiness as he did so. He had long ago become accustomed to the morning nausea ritual. The back of his throat burned from the post nasal drip common to the habitual cocaine user. This was accompanied by the crunching upper nasal passage headache that went with his near nightly use of little blue "pecker pills" that allowed Frank to produce and maintain the erection necessary to have a satisfying night of whoring.

Ah…women. Even more than the drugs and alcohol, Frank Bennington loved women above all things. He loved having them around him, drinking, dancing, and fucking - lots and lots of fucking. He loved the texture of their skin, the warmth of their breath, the sound of their laughter, and their appreciation of how hard he worked to please them in bed.

God was a pretentious, uncaring prick – but Frank forgave Him all of that because He gave the world women! White, black, brown, red, tall, short, thin or fat, Frank Bennington's appetite for all women had been the defining hallmark of his life. After his third failed marriage twelve years ago, he decided to simply enjoy the moments as they came to him, without the ongoing obligations and resulting complications of a legal contract.

Frank stumbled against one of the two dressers in the bedroom of his small Lorin Estates apartment as he walked sans clothing toward the hallway bathroom, causing him to curse under his breath. He glanced back to the bed where the naked form of Silia lay, her dark skin contrasting against the white sheets. In recent months she had become Frank's regular. Her rates were reasonable, and she appreciated that he allowed her to sleep over afterwards. She was twenty seven years old, having come to America from her home country of Brazil four years ago. Other than that, Frank knew little about her, and didn't care to know. Too much of that kind of knowledge brought about emotional ties, and he'd had enough of those already. He just wanted somebody to spend a little time with and then fuck, and Silia happily kept to that arrangement.

Am I supposed to meet someone today? Oh – the new guy! The kid from Ohio.

It was almost 10:00 a.m. He'd told the kid to show up by 8:00. Not wanting to appear completely dysfunctional to the newest member of Congressman Latner's team on the newbie's first day, Frank called down to the apartment lobby.

"Jose, have my car out front in thirty minutes. Thank you."

That left no time for a shower, or even a shave. Frank brushed his teeth, washed his face, and combed his thinning hair back from his forehead. A fresh application of deodorant and cologne, followed by putting on one of the ten freshly starched white dress shirts delivered to him every Monday morning from the Asian, family-owned Van's Dry Cleaning just two blocks from the apartment complex, and his favorite pair of navy blue dress slacks, left Frank almost ready to take on another work day.

In the small single closet of his apartment he kept twenty ties and matching sets of suspenders arranged by color. Yesterday he had worn a dark blue tie and suspenders, so today should be something opposite that. Frank grabbed one of his two pink sets. He had long ago discovered that a man could wear the same clothing one day after the next if all he made certain to do was simply change out his tie and suspenders each time.

Where's my fucking shoes?

Two years ago during his last check-up, Frank's doctor explained to him that the ongoing pain in his feet was due to pre-diabetic neuropathy. It was suggested at that time Frank find a pair of shoes that offered ample arch support to lessen the pain. The same doctor also urged him to lose weight, lessen his drinking, and stop using drugs altogether.

Frank ignored every suggestion but the shoes.

Silia still lay sleeping in the bed, the sound of her soft snoring making Frank smile. Beyond the bed, nightstands, and two thrift store dressers, the room was devoid of furnishings. Silia's clothing lay scattered on the floor, but the only pair of shoes Frank now owned remained hidden.

His headache was getting worse.

Might have left my shoes in the kitchen, along with the coke.

Frank walked down the short hallway to the small kitchen area. His wallet, keys, and Rolex lay on the countertop, as well as a near empty bottle of Wild Turkey, an open, half full bottle of Viagra, and a small plastic bag of cocaine, delivered to him inside one of the Capitol Building bathrooms last week by his longtime supplier Jaxx. Jaxx was the primary hook-up for half the drug users in Congress, which made him a very rich man.

His white running shoes sat on the off white tile of the kitchen floor directly in front of the stainless steel refrigerator. Frank Bennington hadn't gone running since he was a kid, but the shoes made his feet feel better, so he wore them everywhere he went.

"Frank, you leaving already? You wanna fuck again before you go?"

God I love the sound of that voice!

Frank glanced down at his watch, and then wondered if enough of the Viagra he had taken in the early morning hours the night before remained in his system.

"C'mon back to bed Frank...I know you want to."

His headache had lessened some as Frank made his way back to the bedroom where Silia lay above the covers of the bed, her arms and legs, and all her other wonderfully dark toned feminine parts beckoning him to join her.

"I'm running late Silia. Christina is gonna be pissed."

Silia's plump lips formed a pout as she rose up onto her knees and shook her head, causing the long black strands of her hair to fall over her face and full breasts.

"Won't take long - I promise."

Silia stuck a finger into her mouth and looked back at Frank, her dark eyes dancing with seductive mischief.

Frank stood before Silia as she quickly worked the front of his dress slacks loose. He glanced at his watch once again and then placed an appreciative hand behind the Brazilian woman's head as she expertly began to coax his lower half back to life.

"I hate to have to rush you, but you have just five minutes to get this done."

Silia grinned back up at Frank before returning to her work.

She didn't need five minutes...

Printed in Poland
by Amazon Fulfillment
Poland Sp. z o.o., Wrocław